Pull

by

Jaime Winn

PRESS

ISBN 978-1-951796-10-5 (hardcover)
ISBN 978-1-951796-11-2 (paperback)
ISBN 978-1-951796-12-9 (ebook)

Cover design by Tom Anderson

Pull

1

Mischa

These hallways echo, shiny white concrete blocks that are all shadows tonight.

I yank off my heel and throw it behind me into the darkness. I hear it land, but he could still be that close.

Casey has my other hand and is pulling me forward. He catches my shoulder when we skid around the corner of the gym.

"Here," he says, "the stairs."

My feet are slippery now, starting to sweat. I squeeze his hand and balance against his weight when I don't catch the railing right away. I count the stairs then—*Five. Six. Seven.* That's better, isn't it, to count than to think about blood soaking through buttery yellow satin? *Eleven. Twelve.*

There's a loud creak, and Casey pushes me through the door to the boys' locker room. He leads me blindly then between the rows of metal mesh and through the showers. There's a high window at the back, the moonlight shimmering through the frosted glass.

My foot gets caught in my dress as I climb up onto the ledge, and I feel the satin pull around my hips, but my breathing's too loud to hear the tear.

My hands touch the glass, and then Casey's there beside me pushing at the hinges. When I slide my head under the frame, he shoves me forward.

On the other side, a wall of hot air hits me before I can stand up, the dew creeping through the fabric over my knees.

Then we're running again, across the lawn and through the baseball diamond, my feet sucking down into the clipped grass. We don't stop to close the window. We don't look back.

The only lights now are far away, out on Fifth Street, but I imagine I can hear something behind us, that there's more noise beyond my breath and our feet and the swoosh of satin as it gets caught up between my legs.

"You're okay?" Casey asks when we get to the other side of the field, to the chain link fence there.

Once we're still, I can hear the buzzing of the cicadas,

can feel the moisture in the air squeezing my lungs and sticking my dress to me.

"The woods," I tell him, and this is when it hits me that I won't be able to come back to these woods, to the fallen tree where I used to sit on warm afternoons to study with the sun shaking down through the leaves. That's gone for me now. Everything I know will be gone soon.

I hear water running through the irrigation ditch below the fence, but I can't see the bottom of it. I squint down into the darkness as I climb, the chain link digging into my feet.

Somewhere behind us, there's a scream.

Casey jumps down. When I get to the top, all I can see are his hands reaching up out of the darkness.

But I know he's going to catch me, the way I know him beyond reason, beyond explanation.

"Just fall," he says.

And I do.

2

A month before

Do you ever feel like something important is about to happen? Not a specific something, but a general something, a something you don't know at all yet but that you know, somehow, will change everything? That's how I feel looking out into the early spring drizzle that coats the junior parking lot. I can barely see the Centerville High bulldog on the sign over the stadium as the line of cars creeps through the fog towards Fifth Street.

I keep my foot on the brake and redo my ponytail, smoothing the frizz, but some pieces pop back out around my ears. The humidity's almost cold today, and I have to turn the AC off. The clock on my dashboard flashes when I hit the dial—it's been doing that—before the numbers come up. It's almost 3:30. If the line doesn't move soon, I won't make it to the mall before traffic gets bad out by the highway.

Maybe that's why I feel this way now. That's what I tell myself, anyway, that this is excitement and maybe a little anxiety about picking up my prom dress. It was on one of those crazy black Friday sales with free alterations, and I was definitely excited then. Not so much when I went to get it fitted last week. The gray looked so elegant, so sophisticated in November, but now it just looks like all these clouds. It's that heaviness in the air, the way March always feels with its gusty changes and rain and mud.

So this weirdness could just be the pressure changes— my spidey senses, as my mom used to call them, trying to make my lupus into a superpower and that funny, tight feeling right before I'd do something like projectile vomit after too much sun or stress or whatever into something good, something that made me special.

A bunch of cars all go at once, and I almost don't stop in time when the SUV in front of me slams on its breaks.

I look in my rearview, through the windshield of the truck behind me, and lock eyes with Casey Everfeld.

The mall parking lot's almost full by the time I pull in, but I get lucky and find a spot open right outside Lacey's.

Inside, everything's different than last week, racks of dresses all pushed to one side of the store and a big section blocked off by yellow tape. There's a ladder in the taped-off area with a pair of legs disappearing into the ceiling.

It takes me a minute to wind around to the register. The woman there takes my ticket with the number on it and goes behind the changing rooms to get my dress, but she comes back empty-handed just a minute later.

"I'm so sorry," she says, gesturing to ladder. "We sent out emails, but I guess we missed you. There were a few dresses that were ruined in the flood Sunday night."

I tell her mine was fitted last Thursday, but she just apologizes again. They'll refund me, of course, she says, and she'll help me find another dress. There was a pipe that broke in the ceiling, and they couldn't do anything when they found the dresses Monday morning all stained and musty.

"Only a few of them," she says. "I'm sorry you were one of the unlucky ones."

I tell her I understand, that this isn't a big deal; I can always find another dress.

But not for $50, the sale price from Black Friday I was so excited about. The woman's frowning when she gets on the computer. Janet, her nametag says, and she's using my name now, too. Like *I'm so sorry, Mischa. Let me talk to my manager, Mischa. Because unfortunately, Mischa, we don't have any dresses at those prices anymore.*

"I can offer you a full refund and another fifty percent of store credit," she says when she comes back to the register this time. "I know it's just $75, but there's actually something we have that might fit you."

I agree to try it and follow her back to the changing room, where she brings me a yellow satin dress that shimmies over the door and lands in a silky puddle in my hands. The hanger falls through it, and I can't figure out what the neckline looks like until I've pulled it over my ponytail.

My hair tie comes out when I get it on, my hair landing in a mass of frizzy waves over my shoulder as I stare at my reflection in the mirror.

"It was returned," Janet tells me through the door, "but it wasn't one of ours. I think it might be from Macy's. We had a new girl that day on the register, and she didn't know any better than to take it back."

I pull the tag out from under my arm. It's $72.05.

"So it's a big discount," Janet says, "just like Black Friday. But I know it's a long shot. Is it even close to your size? There's a matching wrap that..."

I look back at the mirror. I almost don't recognize myself. It's like I've been supercharged, and by *yellow*. Who knew? This is nothing like the gray.

I reach for my hair tie on the floor and tell Janet this dress is perfect.

The yellow satin's cocooned in plastic on my passenger seat as I drive home. When I pull into the garage and turn down the fan so it doesn't freeze me with AC in the morning, my dash clock flashes again. *72:05.*

I sit back. I must not have seen it right, turned the four into a seven and a two somehow. It hits 4:06 before it goes dark again.

Maybe 7,205's just my lucky number, I joke when I try on the dress for my mom that night.

She doesn't laugh. She asks again how I'm feeling and if I'm stressed with school. She's been worried I haven't been getting enough sleep this semester and keeps saying things about how many AP classes I'm taking. I guess she thinks this must be stress, too, that I've just started to hallucinate numbers now.

But at least she's sold on the dress. "Lucky," she agrees.

3

This is just a memory. I know it even though I'm asleep. I think I should be able to change something like that library book I read on lucid dreaming talked about, but it doesn't matter how hard I try to see the boy handing me the umbrella. There's always a blank spot where his face should be.

I'm nine and at the track for the county schools' shared PET day, waiting outside on a bench instead of trying to cram into the locker rooms under the stadium with all the other kids when it starts to rain. I can hear their voices. Not his, though. I can't make him say anything, can't give him a voice.

He's jogging away already when I turn around—when I turn*ed* around—and he looks back at me with the same missing face.

I focus on the handle of the umbrella he gave me. There's a crack down the middle of the wood and a light patch on the hook where it's been hung somewhere. The shade's green and white with a smudge that looks like runny chocolate from the Dilly bars I used to eat back then.

As I wake up, the umbrella fades away like it always does.

With my eyes open, I go through it all again. I've been having the dream more often lately; it used to only come a couple times a year. I guess this is better than recurrent nightmares, though, than everything I've read about the kind of dreams that won't go away.

I take a sip of water from my nightstand and go back to sleep, and I don't dream of anything else until my alarm goes off at 6:30.

It feels like it takes me longer than usual to get through my morning oatmeal, and the chlorine in the pool hallway's already starting to give me a headache by the time I push through the double doors just before the bell.

Bimi's waiting for me in our usual spot at the end of the hallway. She's chewed a line in her pink lip gloss.

"You said it's *yellow*?" she asks as soon as she sees me.

I follow her towards our lockers.

"Your dress," she prompts as I'm digging my phone out of my purse. "The new one. It's...yellow?" Bimi says 'yellow' like 'meatloaf day.'

I give her my phone and let her flip through the pictures I took of the dress on Friday as we walk towards the English hallway. We're moving too slowly today, it feels like, the impending Bimi fashion judgment hanging in the air like that fruity body mist the cheerleaders wear and whatever spray the football players put all over their abs that smells like creosote.

"Shit," Bimi says, pulling me into a bathroom alcove. "Hang on."

I look over her shoulder as she switches to my Social app and navigates to Kaitlen Miller's page. The picture that loads on the screen then is of a yellow satin-donned Kaitlen, her hair pulled up in one hand as she makes a kissy face at the camera. She's wearing what's unmistakably my new dress, generously padded at the butt and boobs. I look at the timestamp. She posted it three weeks ago.

"Maybe she won't notice," Bimi says after a second, like this might *not* be the straw that triggers the next great Kaitlen Miller meltdown and ricochets off every other cheerleader like drama dominoes.

"Sure," I say.

Bimi bites her lip, scraping off another line of gloss. "What about putting a shawl with it?" she asks.

"It came with one."

"That's something. You could dye it, maybe, and..."

I almost laugh. I don't know why; this won't be funny.

"We'll figure something out," Bimi says when the bell rings. "We'll wrap the shawl weird, like one of those knots Kate Middleton wore her scarf in, and Kaitlen will have her head stuck so far up her padded-out ass she might not even know you're wearing her dress."

The sun's out at the end of the day, so I head to my usual spot in the patch of woods that runs along Fifth Street to wait out the traffic. It's one of those sweet spring afternoons with a cool breeze and none of the sticky humidity from last week. March is always bumpy like this, though, up and down.

I sit for a while on my log, my clogs sucking down into the mud as I finish the last chapters of *The Bell Jar* for Mrs. Stevens' AP English.

I've lost track of the time when the wind picks up. It carries voices from the baseball diamond and the smell of fresh-cut grass with it. It would be sweet, I think, very William Blake children on the green-style in "The Nurse's Song," if Kaitlen Miller's wasn't the loudest voice.

So it feels more "The Tiger," and I remind myself this

isn't the kind of girl I am, scared of the head cheerleader just because we happened to buy the same prom dress. My arms shouldn't be covered in goosebumps as I climb up to the sidewalk leading to the complex.

Kaitlen and her friends haven't noticed me by the time I get to the corner of the field, and I mentally rehearse my speech asking for permission to wear the dress I've already bought in the usual way of beta females towards the middle-bottom of the high school food chain. I tell myself that maybe I'm low enough in this hierarchy that my wearing the dress won't matter. Maybe she'll even take it as a compliment that I copied her if I say that's what I was going for. Kaitlen's offense-flattery continuum is largely gray area.

I've gotten halfway down the side of the field when the crack of a long hit makes me jump. I turn, and my eyes land on Casey Everfeld on the pitcher's mound. He's looking right at me as someone in the outfield catches the ball.

When I get back to my car, I sit for a minute without turning on the engine and focus on my breath. This isn't a running away, I tell myself, or something like a swoon just from eye contact. Except this *is* a running away, obviously, a massive chickening out.

I must have missed text messages coming in. When I get my phone out of my purse, there's a string of them from Bimi—a bunch of fireworks, hearts, and smiley faces with just a single line of text:

Nate Everfeld asked me to prom!

"I'm not stressed," I repeat a few hours later, eyeing my parents over our Monday night tacos. We're consistent like this—Mexican food on Mondays, lasagna on Tuesdays, and so on. All low spice. The way we Kenning-Elliotts spice things up is by rotating chairs for different views of the back yard.

But this is a family thing, not just a lupus thing, how the same foods make it easier to track triggers when I was first diagnosed. My parents actually hung one of those motivational posters on my wall when I was seven, the kind with inspirational pictures and words like 'Determination' and 'Perseverance.' Only mine said 'Consistency.' Because, you know, who wants to be a soaring eagle when you can be a rabbit with consistent bowel movements?

My mom taps her fork on her plate. "I don't know Nate," she says, ignoring as usual my professions of not stressing like she ignores the "ready in just ten minutes" on the packages of macaroni for Wednesday nights and boils the beejezus out of them. "But *Everfeld*. That sounds familiar."

I pick at my taco. It's part of my favorite combo number eight with a cheese quesadilla and a chunk of avocado and sour cream on top. This is a special Mexican night, takeout from Las Palomas—because the local family who built a Mexican restaurant in the old Ruby Tuesday's doesn't speak Spanish and had no idea 'palomas' means 'pigeon.' The Mexican we usually make on Mondays is more bland. So I assume Mom really is trying to coax something more out of me tonight by plying me with a quesadilla and better taco cheese.

"You've probably heard of *Casey* Everfeld," I offer. It seems like everyone has by now from the sports section of our local paper. "He was adopted by that family in middle school."

She waves her fork in a series of circles in front of her face. "That's it," she says. "So, if Bimi..."

"I'm still going to prom," I tell her, chewing a chunk of hardened cheese. But when I look up, both of my parents are studying me like I'm doing something much more telling than eating a taco.

"That's got to be pretty rough for you," Dad says, "with Bimi going with a date now. Do you feel..."

I reassert the non-bothered, non-abandoned, non-stressy

self my parents inevitably disbelieve. Bimi was the same way earlier on the phone, though. She tried to convince me we could keep our pre-prom plans and just hang out with Nate once we got to the dance. I have no idea what vibes I'm giving off that make either my best friend or my parents think I can't handle going to prom by myself. It's like how Mom and Dad were when I started driving and they made me wait until I was almost seventeen to take my driver's test, asking what the big rush was.

"What about your thesis?" Mom asks. "Fourth quarter starts next week, doesn't it?"

I suppress a groan that would inevitably be mistaken for stress. My mom's a devoted reader of the parent newsletters. They have some kind of middle-aged chat room on an ancient server, too, that the school keeps up for parents like her.

"Yep," I say, probably too cheerfully. "I'm excited to start my thesis."

She sets down her fork.

I shovel some more cheese into my mouth. Las Palomas' is chewier, but it tastes better than the kind from the grocery store. Mom's tried half a dozen blends and still hasn't found one that mimics theirs, so our usual Monday tacos are more like meaty pizza cheese meets macaroni cheese on low sodium tortillas.

"You could drop the last quarter of something else so

you'd have a study hall," she says. "Sophie's mom told me she did it. I think it was Psychology she dropped."

When I don't respond, she keeps going on about partial credit and how I don't need any more credits this year, anyway, how I don't need any more *stress* this year than I have already. She hasn't said the *f* word, yet, at least. 'Flare' is roughly equivalent to 'Voldemort' in the Kenning-Elliott household. She tries not to say 'lupus,' too. Because I'm just 'special,' you know. I shouldn't do PE because I'm *special*. I shouldn't go to the amusement park with my friends in the summers because I'm *special*. I should maintain a complete, descriptive log of all my bowel movements because I'm *special*.

I tell her I'll think about dropping a class, because the appeasing teenager card is always a winner, and finally, she goes back to picking at her tamale.

"Bigger things," my dad says when it's been quiet for a while. It's what they've always said, that I have bigger things ahead of me. I think it's the Kenning-Elliott version of *hakuna matata*.

"Bigger things," I echo.

4

With all the electronics buzzing around me in the computer lab Wednesday morning, I wonder if there's some chance my mom's right and I really could be stressed. I remembered my dreams again this morning, the umbrella memory and then some flashes of places I don't know and people I don't recognize. Mrs. Stevens would probably have something to say about the umbrella, at least. In literature, umbrellas are always penises. But so are swords and trees. Literature is full of penises.

I've been staring out the window for a while when the lunch bell rings and I remember I haven't signed up for a thesis section yet.

When I open the box with the search bar and enter my student ID, all that loads is a section search by number. I check my bag for the catalog, but I must have left it in my locker.

I look back at the screen. There's space for four digits.

I try *1234.*

A box pops up with *Section not found.*

I pause for just a second before I type *7205.*

The screen goes black. *Section confirmed,* it says then, with Mrs. Stevens' classroom number.

"You'll come on Saturday?" Bimi asks a few minutes later while we're waiting in the a la carte line for pizza.

I look back at her just as some fries are being emptied into the tray in front of me—waffle fries today, extra greasy. "Saturday?" I ask.

Bimi gives me that distinctive Bimi look that says she's just been talking about this. But she's been talking since we got in line, and I thought it was all about Nate—*hunk of Nateness* now. He's rapidly evolving.

"The game," she prompts.

"Baseball?" I guess it's fresh in my mind after going to the field the other day. "Nate plays?" I ask.

Bimi sighs, dropping an orange onto her tray and gesturing to the pizza when the lunch lady brings out a fresh box. "Casey," she tells me.

"Oh." I wonder if she said his name before. I think it

would have caught my attention. So I try to pretend this hasn't caught my attention now and sound as bored as possible when I form his name as a question. "Casey?"

Bimi nods. "So Nate and I are gonna go watch."

"Like a date."

Bimi wobbles her head back and forth like the hula bobblehead glued to her dashboard. "We'll get dinner after, but his parents'll be at the game, like I said. So you should come. It's just casual."

"Casual," I echo. But Bimi sounds anything *but* casual about Nate Everfeld/hunk of Nateness. Not that Bimi's ever been casual about anything else, either; I think she was born with one of those 'Determination' posters on her wall and it really took hold of her early on. Though I picture Bimi less as a peacefully soaring eagle and more as a strong-willed vulture with carefully-applied makeup that gives her the coloring of an toucan.

The lunch lady—Cathleen, the nice one who always checks the pizza boxes for the good slices for us—drops a big slice of plain cheese onto my tray, and I thank her and follow Bimi to the register to swipe our IDs. Our group's at the usual table with our seats open, but I can see there's an empty seat at the table behind ours, too, where Casey and Nate sit with Kaitlen Miller and some of the other baseball guys and cheerleaders. The youth pastor who's always hanging around them is there today, too.

"So you and Nate are dating," I say, "not just going to prom."

"After Saturday," Bimi confirms, grabbing some napkins out of the dispenser.

"Are you sitting at his table, then?"

She shakes her head. "Not this week." She pauses a table away from ours. "Maybe next week," she says. "You'll come with me, won't you?"

I mumble something noncommittal before we sit down. She hasn't said anything to the others yet about Nate or prom.

But as we listen to Kirsten's newest little-sister-being-a-beauty-queen drama, I catch her sending smiles at her hunk of Nateness between bites of pizza and know this has already surpassed anything we could call 'casual.'

I must be thinking about baseball that night when I go to bed. I dream I'm at the field watching Casey Everfeld on the pitcher's mound.

He's about to pitch when he spins around and throws to third base, instead. The crowd's loud then, and a runner who was trying to steal third jogs off the field.

I'm still looking at Casey when the dream fades, and I

spend all of Econ and a long Bio lab Thursday morning wondering why I can't get Casey Everfeld out of my head.

*   *

Saturday welcomes April with storm clouds that don't run out of rain until right before the game's supposed to start.

I wait at home for too long, thinking it should be canceled, but the sun's peeking through the clouds by the time I'm turning off the radio just after the sports guy announces the first pitch—Casey Everfeld again.

I call Bimi once I'm out the door. "I'll be there by next quarter," I tell her.

"Inning," she says.

"Inning," I correct, and agree to meet her by the concession stand.

It really is the next inning, I think—the players are all running around—when I finally make it up to the field from the lower lot, trying to keep my focus anywhere but on the pitcher's mound.

The sky's gone cotton candy, the storm clouds brightening to oranges and pinks in the later innings. But there are more rolling in that look the same dark gray of the

Linsville Eagles' uniforms, and I think I can hear that rumbling kind of April thunder in the distance.

Casey looks up at us as he heads to the dugout for the last time. That's one word, 'dugout.' His dad—Nate's dad, at least, Rick Everfeld—came to sit by me as soon as I got here and has been teaching me baseball talk whenever there's a break in the game or the Bulldogs are batting. He can't concentrate on anything else when Casey's on the pitcher's mound. But neither can anyone else.

"So you dating anybody, Mischa?" Rick asks after our first batter's out. The game's tied now.

"*Rick!*" Ellen, his wife, yells over Bimi and Nate.

Rick rolls his eyes.

Bimi glances at me but keeps talking in that steady, excited hum she's kept up with Nate all through the game. It's occasionally punctuated by cheers when something happens on the field, but her focus is obviously on the hunk of Nateness on her other side.

"I was just asking," Rick says. "That's what you young people do, isn't it, 'dating' or is it 'talking' now? It's not 'going steady' anymore, is it?"

Ellen yells an apology my way and throws up her hands.

"No," I offer when I realize Rick's still waiting for an answer. "I'm not..." What is it? *Speak the teenager, Mischa!* "I'm not dating anyone."

Rick sits up and cranes his neck to see down into the dugout. "Huh," he says.

"*Rick*," Ellen repeats.

Bimi glances at me, twitching her nose. But she has that special, no-makeup-can-match Bimi glow blooming over her cheeks and seems to lose interest in my dating habits as soon as Nate says something in her other ear.

The Bulldogs are ahead by one—and only one—in the second half of the last inning. It's like the whole crowd's holding their breath then, but Casey looks calm when he steps onto the pitcher's mound.

"He's always like that," Rick tells me. "Kid can keep his cool through anything." Because Casey's special, too, Rick keeps saying, in case I might not have noticed. Special in a strong way, though, in a get-out-there-and-smush-some-Eagles way, not special in a wrap-you-in-bubble-wrap-and-feed-you-bland-food way, like my parents think I am.

I mumble something like I know this, like I know *him*, and then I'm quiet with the rest of the crowd as the first batter for the Eagles steps up to the plate.

There's one out and runners on first and second when Casey spins around and throws the ball to third. I know it just a second before he does it. It's exactly the way it happened in my dream.

The crowd roars around me then. Bimi and Rick are both on their feet yelling. It takes me a second to stand up.

The runner who was trying to steal third jogs back to the Eagles' dugout, and then an outfielder catches the next hit and the cheering just keeps going until I can't hear myself think anymore.

Afterwards, I wait in my car as the rain pours down in sheets of shimmering navy against the sea of taillights trying to get out to Fifth Street.

I breathe in for four, hold for four, breathe out for four, hold for four, the way my pediatrician taught me when I was twelve. Like this really is stress, really is normal, the way dreams sometimes happen in real life.

I told myself I'd only wait here until some of the traffic had cleared out, all the beeping horns and the yelling out cracked windows. Before that, I told myself I'd leave as soon as I couldn't see Bimi and Nate anymore as they made a run for the pizza place down the street, holding an umbrella between them. And before that, I told myself I'd go as soon as I'd caught my breath. I shouldn't have needed to catch my breath just walking away from a baseball game with Ellen's red umbrella pressing down over my hair—so I'd be easy to see the rain, she said, since I insisted I didn't need a ride to my car.

I don't remember when it got dark, and as I start the engine—maybe I should have done that before, too—cold air blasts out through the vents and leaves my arms prickled in goosebumps.

I look at my dashboard clock and wait for the numbers to come, but it doesn't even flash this time. The lot's empty when I finally pull out and head towards Fifth Street.

I see lightning in the distance at the same time I blow past the intersection, but I don't see the white truck until after we've already hit.

And maybe this is another dream, I tell myself when I know it's Casey before I see his face, before I can even make out the uniform coming towards me in another flash of lightning. Rain's running down his jacket and darkening his hair.

I roll down my window, but he's already around the hood and opening my passenger door.

"Are you okay?" he asks when he gets inside.

"I'm sorry," I say automatically, still looking out the windshield, at the rain sparking in his headlights.

He's still for a second before he pulls his door closed,

and then it's quiet inside.

"I didn't see you," I tell him, and "I'm sorry" again. I don't know what else to say. Because I'm awake, you know, and I have no idea how I conjured Casey Everfeld in my car on a rainy April Saturday night.

Warm air's hissing louder through the vents now.

"There's a dent on your bumper," Casey says when it feels like we've been quiet for too long. "A little one. I can get it out."

And then it's a plan before I can think to get away. Before I can think at all, really. I'll follow Casey in his truck to a gas station that's been out of business for years by the bypass that leads out to Lincoln. He'll know what to do from there, he says.

I know I should tell him I'll go home, instead, that I'll get to a garage later, that I'll go wherever I have to, with anyone but him. But I don't. I just watch as he closes my door and jogs back to his truck. Then I follow his taillights out to the bypass.

The parking lot's dark and empty. I can't remember what the gas station that used to be here was called, but I can still picture the fat pink bubblegum squares they kept in a glass jar by the register. I feel like I can taste them in the dampness and can smell the fake grapes and cherries of the suckers on the peg board on the wall, too. The painted blue letters have peeled off the side of the building now, and as I pull in behind Casey, my headlights catch some ivy climbing up the concrete wall where the restrooms used to be.

He parks next to me and leaves his door open so there's a warm puddle of light from his dash that covers the asphalt between us. I get out and step into it. Everything else is gone then, faded into the darkness through a curtain of mist. The rain's just a patter now around the rectangle of the overhang, a soft drizzle that gurgles as it drains down into the woods.

Casey's bending over my bumper when I turn back to him, and it takes me a while to think of something to say.

"So you're not going to kill me now, are you, for hitting your truck?" I ask, trying for a laugh when I don't think I can be quiet anymore.

I wait for him to laugh, too, but he doesn't. I guess my voice didn't come out right.

"I *am* sorry," I tell him. "I should have been paying attention. I don't know why I wasn't."

"It's fine," he says. "As long as you're okay?"

"I'm okay," I confirm, and he turns back to the hood.

After a minute, he tells me he's sure can get this out—it's a dent he's pointing to that he says looks bigger than it really is, if I saw it from a different angle. I don't go around to get a better look at it. I don't move at all.

He gets some things from his truck before coming back and kneeling on the concrete.

I tell him that I can go to a garage, but he waves me off. I'd forgotten his parents—not his parents, I guess, properly, but the Everfelds—have the big dealership out on Second Avenue where he works over the summers. Bimi told me that. It stuck out in one of her long hunk of Nateness soliloquies, how that's when Nate and Casey got close, that first summer after the Everfelds adopted him in middle school when the two of them started doing odd jobs at the dealership.

I almost ask Casey about this, about what it's like to work on cars or to get a new family. But I don't know what's off limits or stupid or wrong, so it's just our breaths and the patter of rain between little dings of a hammer as he taps out the dent.

I'm about to say something about the weather (*the weather, Mischa!*) when his voice interrupts my not-so-eloquent thoughts on storms and something about magnetism I should remember better from my Earth Science class last semester.

"I didn't know you liked baseball," he says.

Of course. Baseball. I could have said something about

the game. I mean, I was there. I saw him win. *Them* win. It just felt like him winning.

"You were...that was good, the last inning," I say, because I know innings now. I just have to not think about how I saw the important part of that particular inning twice.

He glances over his shoulder at me, but his face is in a shadow. "You were there for Bimi," he says, not really asking.

I nod. "She and Nate seem..." I try to find the word. Maybe it's too early for 'happy,' but I say it anyway.

"Nate is," Casey says.

"That's great."

"Yeah."

I listen to the rain for a couple more minutes, and then he stands, running his hand over the bumper.

"Should be good now," he says. "Like nothing happened."

"Like nothing happened," I echo as a soft roll of thunder cuts through the quiet. I thank him again. The air's thick still, a hint of heat left behind from the storm even as the breeze goes through my jacket.

"It's no problem," Casey says. He waits until I'm in my car to get in his truck.

I take a second to get myself settled and look again at my dashboard clock. I think I see a flash there, but no numbers show up.

Casey's truck doesn't pull out behind me until I'm on the road heading back to town.

5

Casey

Monday's the first day of fourth quarter, and I get to Thesis early. Mischa should be here in Mrs. Stevens' section. She's into English.

I look at the empty desk next to mine. Matt Walters was there for a while until Lori Durchol called him to come sit by her across the room. And lucky thing, too; he made Kaitlen Miller take the desk in front of mine, and at least she can't stay turned around backwards talking at me all quarter. She's twisted in the other direction and hasn't noticed yet that he moved.

I keep looking at the door. But I know Mischa was in Stevens' AP English; she'd want to write a paper instead of give a talk, I think. I could have asked her. I *should* have asked her. I had the chance to on Saturday. I look at the clock again. It's only a minute till.

The-Kaitlen-who-won't-shut-up is going on about her project. She's got it all figured out and suggests we write our papers together. I don't know what she thinks I'm doing mine on; she hasn't asked.

I see Mischa's binder—the big padded purple one that zips up, the one she's had for a while—before she's fully in the doorway. She looks at me, but then her eyes dart around the room. I gesture to the empty desk. It's about her only option now, and she sits down.

I don't pay attention to Kaitlen or to whatever Mrs. Stevens is writing on the board or to the bell or to anything, really, but Mischa sitting next to me. I don't get a chance to say anything to her, but I notice whenever she writes something down, when she fiddles with her pencil or taps an eraser on her desk, when she shifts around in her chair, the way I've noticed everything about Mischa Kenning-Elliott since I first walked into the Centerville complex in seventh grade and saw her across the hall.

6

Mischa

Tuesday in the lunch line, Bimi gives me a bite-by-bite account of her pizza date after Saturday's game with Hunk of Nateness—capitalized at this point, I think, very official. Because he's *her* Hunk of Nateness now, a proper noun ensconced for the second day in a row at our lunch table. They'll switch off, she tells me, but it doesn't really matter whose table they're sitting at; they're fully engrossed in each other.

I guess they're in that melding phase that's expected now, sharing tables and stories they never seem to run out of and acclimating to each other in the little ways, her swapping her heels for flats—she already has some satin slippers she found to match her prom dress—and wearing her hair lower to match his height, him planning a trip to the mall with her Saturday afternoon to get a corresponding blue vest for his tux. They'll have a fancy dinner at the Italian place by the highway afterwards.

So I'm not surprised when she's immediately sucked into conversation with him when we sit down. She tries to include me when she remembers to, and I'm mostly following Nate's preference for eggplant over all the spaghetti options at Bella Vista when Casey joins his usual crowd at the table behind ours and his voice starts intruding. Because my brain's looking for him, I guess, after the game and sitting next to him in Thesis.

The youth pastor dominates conversation at that table again. Casey doesn't say much, and Pastor Dave's loud, his voice carrying like he wants to be heard. I try to tune him out, and I think I'm doing a pretty good job of it until I hear him say 'synchronicities' a second time.

"...and that's how you know," he says, pausing for one of Kaitlen's boob-heaving gasps. "That's how you know you're under the influence of the occult."

I listen as he talks about how it starts, how things just seem to line up, how you get feelings of *deja vous* — even though he doesn't pronounce it correctly—how outside forces, *evil* forces, start influencing you, sometimes through your dreams.

Bimi taps my leg under the table. I look up, breaking off a staring contest with my pizza crust.

"Sorry," I say.

"I was just telling h..." She almost says *Hunk of Nateness.* She clears her throat. "Nate," she says, resting a hand on his arm. "I was just telling Nate that Bella Vista's good with you."

"Uh huh," I say, then, "What?"

She gives me the Bimi eye. *"For prom,"* she says.

My elbow lands in my pizza, and I go through my usual string of protests then, telling her they should go wherever they want, that I'll catch up with them after at the dance. I definitely don't need to third wheel their romantic dinner; I can easily see this becoming a *Lady and the Tramp* situation over spaghetti even if Nate thinks now that he prefers eggplant.

Nate goes from nodding, his near-constant state around Bimi, to shaking his head in time with her.

"We'll figure that out later," she says, wrinkling her nose.

I agree and, when it seems like I should say something else, I ask Hunk of Nateness if Bimi's told him about her new prom slippers.

I dawdle at my locker, organizing my books for tomorrow before heading to Mrs. Stevens' room for Thesis. Casey's already there when I get in. The bell rings just as

I'm sitting down.

There's a bunch of stuff up on the board today that I start writing in my notebook. Now I can almost think it's lucky that I ended up in the right section from the random number I entered in the computer. Or that it *would* have been lucky, anyway, if the number had been random. I hadn't read the catalog and didn't know the sections all have different themes, different requirements, but this one's perfect for me—a paper comparing and contrasting ideas from two pieces of literature. Because they're more interesting in pairs, Mrs. Stevens always says.

Kaitlen's hand shoots up as soon as the rubric's on the board. "But I want to do the occult," she says before Mrs. Stevens has even turned around. "A study of it."

Stevens takes a deep breath, and I hope this time that she might use it to blow Kaitlen out of her seat like the big, bad wolf. Coincidentally, *The Three Little Pigs* is possibly the most sophisticated piece of literature Kaitlen's made it all the way through. She and a couple other cheerleaders did a sexy rendition of it for the drama festival last year. I assume she picked this section for Casey.

"And your pieces of literature?" Mrs. Stevens asks.

Kaitlen slumps. "…'Hamlet,' maybe?" she says. "With the witches?"

"'Macbeth,'" Casey offers. "You mean 'Macbeth.'"

I turn to look at him. So does Mrs. Stevens.

"...*and*," she prompts after a second.

Kaitlen shrugs.

Mrs. Stevens moves on when some others raise their hands with questions. I watch Casey out of the corner of my eye, but he doesn't say anything else. "Macbeth," though. He must have taken Stevens' Shakespeare class and just been in a different section than I was. That's why he's here then, instead of with the other jocks doing group scenes or whatever they're slacking off on in the theater.

We have a while at the end of the period to fill out a preliminary bibliography and a topic proposal. I'm ready for this, and I fill up both sides of the page quickly. I spent last semester on short stories and want to do Edgar Allan Poe's "The Tell-Tale Heart" and Charlotte Perkins Gilman's "The Yellow Wallpaper," two narrators who seem like they're different kinds of crazy.

Not because *I'm* crazy, I want to write at the end of the proposal, or because I think I might be moving in that direction. At least no one's messing with me like Gilman's narrator, and I'm not justifying killing anyone like Poe's. That has to be worth something. I'm only stuck on a number and having some weird dreams. Hardly the stuff of madness.

The bell's just rung, but I have a free period at the end

of the day on Tuesdays since I've already taken the SAT, so I wait for Mrs. Stevens to read through my notes.

"Interesting," she says when she's finished. "Really interesting idea, Mischa. I like it." But she's looking behind me.

When I turn around, Casey's there. I hurry by him, but he hands in his paper and catches up with me by the time I get to the front of the room.

He follows me through the door. "Can I walk with you?" he asks.

I stop. The hallway's quiet; passing period's over. "I'm done for the day," I tell him, pointing down the hall to the atrium that leads out to the junior lot.

He nods and falls into step beside me. We pass a science class with Mrs. Kinwell's voice coming through the open door and then one of the tech rooms with a saw buzzing.

"You have a minute?" Casey asks when we get to the atrium.

I nod and force myself to stop. I don't know what I'm afraid of, what's causing this shaking inside my body when I'm just standing in a sunny atrium with Casey Everfeld. It's not like he could know my thoughts, like he could know my dreams. Maybe that's it, though, that I think he *can* know somehow, that he might see through me.

I feel a blush warming my cheeks and tell myself how stupid this is. Of course he can't read my mind. And this shouldn't be a lupus trigger; I don't have a reason to lobster up now. He probably just wants me to talk Bimi out of going to prom with Nate or something, like anyone could talk Bimi out of anything.

I take a step back, and my heel hits one of the potted plants, shaking the big fan-like leaves over our heads.

"I was wondering if we could hang out sometime," Casey says.

"Hang out," I echo. My tongue sticks to the roof of my mouth on the *t*.

He shakes his head. "That's not..." He doesn't finish.

I look up at the leaves.

"I want to get to know you better," he says.

It takes me a while to respond, or maybe it just feels like it. I think of a lot of words in the meantime, because I'm almost sure I know how this should go, the things I should say now. *No.* It's this, isn't it? *No thank you? No, and I think you might have me confused with someone else?* But these words don't come out.

"Okay," is what I say in the end, and it comes out weak and shaky. I clear my throat and am about to say something about spring allergies when I look at him again.

He's smiling. And Casey Everfeld's smile could stop a dagger-wielding Juliet. *Get it together, Mischa.* But I don't get it together.

"Okay," Casey says.

We take a couple steps towards the doors. They feel so freaking far away. Our footsteps are loud on the tile.

"Saturday?" he asks. "Maybe we could go for a walk?"

I nod and focus on keeping my feet moving towards the doors, one in front of the other.

"I see you in the woods sometimes after school," he says. "You walk around behind the sports complex sometimes, don't you?"

"I...sometimes."

"Maybe we could go in the afternoon? I have a curfew cause Sunday's game's early. So I can't be out that late."

I nod again, watching the tiles passing under our feet.

"So Saturday," he says. "The seventh."

"The seventh," I say. We stop by the doors, and I don't want to look up. I swear I can hear the big clock on the wall above us ticking, the second hand chugging along. When I do look up, it's 2:05. *7,205*, my brain echoes.

I shake my head and try to shake all this away. Maybe the whole thing's a dream. Maybe that's why it all feels like it goes together. Writing on a theme, as Mrs. Stevens would say, like my life and my dreams have just gone a little dystopian. And, you know, dreamy.

But Casey's smiling. And then *I'm* smiling, because I can't help it, as I push through the doors and out into the sun. My body feels like it's buzzing when I get to my car, but these are butterflies in my stomach, I think, not ravens. Not like Poe's, not foreshadowing death. And then I don't think of Poe or Gilman for the rest of the night.

7

Casey

Wednesday and Thursday are weird. Not bad weird, but different. My body feels like it's getting ready for a fight or something.

By Friday, Coach Greene's decided it's a good change. It seems to be good for my pitching arm, anyway; I hit 94 mph yesterday at practice. *Instinct*, he said, that my instincts are really kicking in. But I'm pretty sure it's nausea, not instinct, as I'm staring at Stevens' door at the beginning of sixth period waiting for a girl to come through it like my life depends on her getting here before the bell.

Since I asked her Tuesday in the atrium, Mischa hasn't brought up tomorrow. But maybe she hasn't had the chance to. I thought we'd get to talk more; Bimi and Nate pushed the ends of our tables together over lunch, so she sits across from me now, but it's hard to say anything over them, even with the Kaitlen-who-won't-shut-up farther away at the cheerleader's table selling cookies for the football team again. Mischa's friends still look at me like I don't belong at their table, so she must not have said anything to them about tomorrow.

Thesis hour's been all presentations, so I don't have much chance to talk to her in class, either, and then we go in different directions afterwards. We've had practice every day after school, and it's been raining, so she's been heading home instead of sitting out in the woods like she usually does.

Today, Kaitlen's going on about some thing at her church when Mischa finally walks through the door.

But I'm just saying "Hey"—a start, at least—when Kaitlen catches her attention, instead.

"You're coming to church tomorrow, aren't you?" Kaitlen asks her.

My head snaps back to Katilen. She shrugs at me. "You get points," she tells me, "for everybody you bring."

I almost ask her what points are, at a church, but I look at Mischa, instead. *No*, the voice in my head tries to tell her, imagining her stuck in a church full of Kaitlens. *Just say no.*

But she's not looking at me. "It's at night?" she asks. So after our date, she means, since I have a curfew. If it's a date. It probably isn't a date.

"Eight," Kaitlen says.

I stare at Mischa, trying to get her to look at me. *Here, Mischa Mischa*, my head voice calls in the same tone I use when I'm calling Bertie, the Everfelds' goldendoodle. But you can't call girls like goldendoodles. Girls probably don't love you for scraps of table meat, either. I laugh. And then she finally does look at me. Shit.

"Sorry," I say. "You really want to go to that?"

She looks at Kaitlen again, then nods.

"Okay," I say, ignoring Kaitlen's squeal. "I'll ask about curfew."

"So it's a *church* thing?" Ellen asks that night as she's making dinner. Nate's upstairs texting with Bimi. Rick'll have to drag him down to eat.

"It's like a teen..." I search for Kaitlen's word. Now I'm searching for Kaitlen words. No wonder Mischa hasn't told her friends about going out with me. "Shindig?"

Ellen raises her eyebrows as she drains a skillet full of brussel sprouts. Rick groans from the table and mumbles something about cheese. He's been having to watch his cholesterol and I think dreams of mozzarella most nights.

"Who invited you?" Ellen asks.

"Kaitlen Miller."

Rick groans again, either at cheese-free brussel sprouts

or at Kaitlen Miller.

"Sorry," he says when I look over. "But she's..."

"Not my date," I finish for him.

Ellen spins around, dropping a brussel sprout on the floor. "Date?" she asks.

I whistle for Bertie, who comes skidding around the corner, probably expecting meat. But it seems like everybody's going to be disappointed tonight.

Except Ellen, maybe. Ellen's still looking at me. "*Date*?" she repeats. Because I guess I haven't dated in a while. Not really, anyway. Not ever that mattered.

"I...I'm not sure if it's a date," I admit.

"Who with?" Rick asks.

"I know I have Sunday's game," I say, "and I don't think Nate'll want to come to the church thing. He and Bimi..."

"Yeah, yeah, mall, fancy dinner, we know," Rick says. "So who's your date?"

"It might not be a date. We're just going for a walk before..."

"Who?" Ellen interrupts, ignoring Bertie spitting up the brussel sprout into a puddle of cholesterol-safe "butter" on the tile.

"Mischa Kenning-Elliott."

Ellen slams her fist on the counter. "I knew it," she

says. "I knew it."

"I called it first," Rick says.

Ellen's smiling when she brings our plates over to the table. "You know you'll need to wash your truck if you're driving her," she says, because she's Ellen. "Or you could take Rick's car. And what are you wearing?"

They're still talking about Mischa when Nate finally comes down for dinner. Ellen's barely paying attention when he asks if he can go to Bimi's tonight to watch a movie—so they have something to talk about at Bella Vista tomorrow, I guess, like his phone hasn't been dinging all week and he and Bimi could have possibly not covered every topic on the planet over lunch periods.

"Fine," Ellen says, then, "Will Mischa be there?"

"Mischa?" Nate stabs at some chicken with his fork and shovels it into his mouth. "Huh uh."

"But you know her," Rick says.

"We've been sitting with them at lunch," I offer.

Ellen nods. "Good," she says. "So you know her pretty well already."

Nate looks at me, but his mouth's full. He's been so caught up with Bimi, I doubt he could even tell them what Mischa looks like.

"Casey," Rick prompts.

"Uuh?" Nate says through his food.

"I know her a...a little," I say.

Ellen frowns when Nate ejects a mostly chewed ball of chicken. His mouth stays open as he gawks at me from across the table.

"Who?" he asks.

"Mischa Kenning-Elliott," Ellen says. "You didn't know that..."

"Bimi hasn't said anything?" I interrupt. We're all looking at Nate now. I try to swallow a brussel sprout. Mischa definitely doesn't think this is a date if she hasn't even told Bimi.

"I..." Nate's eyes dart back and forth between me and his parents. "I'm sure she..." he starts, then takes a sip of water. "That's great, and...you mean Mischa?"

"Yes," I say at the same time Rick does.

"Right," Nate says. "I mean, I didn't see that coming, but...yeah. Great."

Ellen suggests I call her to settle plans for tomorrow, but I don't have her number.

"You set up a date and didn't ask for the girl's number?" Rick asks.

But Ellen's ahead of him. She tells Nate to get it for me from Bimi when he's over there tonight.

"Early," she clarifies, "and text it right away."

I don't know whether to apologize to Nate or thank him. I end up thanking him.

He shakes his head. "Better get going, then," he says, winking at me as he shovels in another bite of chicken and pushes back his chair.

I go up to my room a little while after Nate's left for Bimi's. I try to read one of the books I want to use for my thesis, a biography of Marlowe, while I wait for him to text, but I'm not absorbing any of it. I'm rereading page three when he finally sends a series of digits.

Did Bimi say anything? I ask. *Like if Mischa told her about tomorrow?*

Want me to ask?

No, I tell him, *but thanks. Have fun.*

He sends back that smiley face with hearts in the eyes, and I swear it looks just like him. Nate's always like that, always starry-eyed over some girl. Though Bimi already seems more serious than the others.

I save Mischa's number in my contacts, and it takes me a while of staring at her name on my screen to finally press the call button. I chicken out and end it before it can connect, then open a text chat, instead.

My phone goes dark while it's waiting for me to finish

some variation of *Are we still on for tomorrow?* I change it a few times before I give up and press send. Because I'm not gonna sound smart to Mischa. Or cool. Or anything else I want to.

She reads it right away. The little dots start bouncing around to say she's typing, and I press the screen twice to keep it from going dark.

Is four okay? she asks. *At the park?*

Perfect, I tell her. *And I can do the church thing after if you still want to go.*

Okay, she says.

Okay, I say. I type, *So it's a date,* then erase. Because it's probably not a date for her. *I'm happy to finally get to talk to you,* I write after a minute and send this before I can change my mind.

8

Mischa

I think when I get to the park that Casey's not actually going to show up, that some giggling Kaitlen Miller type is about to jump out from behind a tree and tell me this was all a joke. Because it would be funny, to a Kaitlen Miller type, Casey Everfeld spending time with someone like me.

I'm twenty minutes early because I didn't know how to get ready. This isn't like a first date, or at least it doesn't feel like the first dates I've been on before, like preparing to barely talk to someone you might have a little crush on through a movie or hanging out together with friends. This is different. Even before the dreams, I think this would have been different.

I check my hair in the rearview mirror and run a brush through it a few times. It's still frizzy. It's been this way all day, though, full of electricity like when I put my hand on that big electrostatic ball at the Magic House on my sixth birthday.

I turn off my car but wait inside it for a while, looking at my phone and pretending something might pop up there worth reading. I finally get out and go stand by the trash cans, swatting away a bee that keeps getting too close. I don't know what to do with my hands, what I'll do when Casey pulls in—*if* Casey pulls in. Since standing doesn't feel right, I walk to a bench that looks over the parking lot.

"Mischa."

I spin around. He's behind me, and I jump up right as my butt's about to land on the bench. It takes me a second to say something then. "You're early," is what comes out. Because I didn't see him coming.

"You, too," he says.

I try to come up with something to say back, something clever.

"You want to walk?" he asks when I don't come up with anything at all.

I start walking. There's no one here today, and the path's quiet. Too quiet. I guess it's all the rain that left mud streaked across the asphalt. I almost say this about the rain, but I was supposed to be more witty than the weather, wasn't I?

For a while, we just walk. Our footsteps are loud, but we don't have anything to say to each other. So I guess this isn't instant chemistry or whatever it is in books or movies, how the characters are talking nonstop at this point and laughing, and right at the beginning, they feel like they've known each other for forever. You can always tell by the time they get to the end of the song montage. By the time we get to the pond on the other side of the park, I guess, for us. But we're still quiet.

Maybe I should have expected this; we never talked before Tuesday, and we don't have anything in common except my best friend and his adoptive brother dating now. So I don't know why I feel like something's pulling my body towards his, why I can't keep my feet in a line on the path, why the back of my hand runs into his sometimes like I'm always falling towards him a little. It's like the world just tilts in Casey's direction, like this is a gravitational thing.

When I feel like I can't stand the quiet any longer, I ask what I already know about his curfew and whether the Everfelds said he could go to the church thing.

"Yeah," he says, then, "if you still want to go."

I nod. Maybe it's because of him, because Kaitlen's part of his group, that I suddenly want to be accepted into it. I'm pretty sure this is all about Casey, all some kind of sneaky obsession on my side that I shouldn't have, that there's no social basis for.

I'm thinking about this when we have to turn around by the pond. I can see the hood of his truck through the bushes in front of that lot. It's weird that I recognize his truck now, I think, that I've seen it every day at school since last week's game.

"You parked over here?" I ask.

He stops on the concrete patch by the duck food dispenser. I don't know where all the ducks are today; the pond's quiet, too.

"I wanted to walk some before," Casey says, looking up at a lone runner rounding the other side of the pond.

So this is where I turn around and go back to my car and he goes to his. But neither of us move.

"Have you walked too much?" he asks. "I could drive you back."

"No," I say, and I wonder if he can tell my heart's beating too fast for just walking. But this isn't lupus, isn't too much sun or cardio. This is something else.

When I turn around, Casey stays with me.

I think we're used to the quiet, that we're just going to keep going like this, when he says, "Would you say something?"

I'm coming up with a retort—I really am. A good one—when I look at him, and it's his face that stops me.

He looks away. "Sorry," he says, then, "I'm not good at this."

I nod, because maybe I'm not good at this, either, even if I thought I was okay at this before, or not *this* before, but that I was okay at whatever I thought this was with other people. I thought I could chatter, at least. It's supposed to be easier when you're nervous, isn't it?

"Bimi and Nate are probably on their way to Bella Vista now," I try.

"Yeah," Casey says after another couple steps. "He was looking forward to it."

"Bimi, too."

"Good."

I nod. We keep walking.

"They're going to prom together," he says.

"She's excited. They're...I think he got a vest today. To match her dress."

"Yeah," he says, "blue."

There's a second of quiet before we both burst out laughing. I don't know what prompts this, but I can't help it. Maybe he can't, either.

We keep laughing for a while—really laughing, the kind that's all air and not much sound, that hurts my stomach even though it isn't loud.

"I'm sorry," he says afterwards, when I'm catching my

breath and sparkles are swimming in the corners of my eyes. The runner passes on our left, looking over like there's some great joke between us.

"No," I say. "It was me."

Casey stops and turns to look at me. "You're okay?" he asks. "Are you uncomfortable, or..."

"No."

He smiles, and we keep walking. And maybe that's all that matters now, that we keep walking.

We've walked back and forth to the pond five times when Casey asks if I want to get dinner before the church thing, since it's getting late. So we leave the path at his parking lot, and I climb up into his truck.

"You like the diner," he says. "That one out on Ferguson. Sallee's?"

I tell him I do.

"Bimi told Nate," he offers after a second.

I look out the window as we pass by my lot and he turns left onto Main. So I guess he's driving us.

I tell him we don't have to go to Sallee's, that I'm not very picky, but he says he isn't, either. So that's where we go, to the place in the old IHOP that's trying to be retro with the pink rope lights over the booths and the waitresses in big skirts with poodles on them. The one who seats us calls us cutie patooties, and I look at Casey to see how he takes this. He's smiling—a real smile, I think, like maybe he's going to laugh again.

We at least make it through our orders without laughing. He gets a sandwich, and I get eggs, the same number I always get here because breakfast food is supposed to be soothing, isn't it, when your stomach feels like mine does now? It's weird to have something other than lupus butterflies for once.

The waitress leaves, taking our menus. I have to look at Casey then, when he's not just a disembodied voice walking along next to me or sitting behind a piece of laminated plastic, and this makes me talk, I guess finally turns on my nervous chatter switch when I don't have anywhere else to look but at the funny way the pink lights glow in his hair.

So I tell him more about Bimi, because this is a safe topic—how excited she is about Nate, how much she was looking forward to their dinner tonight, how she always gets the beef stroganoff at Bella Vista even though she ends up taking half of it home with her because she eats so much bread and olive oil waiting for her food to come.

Then he's talking, too, about Nate. We still laugh every now and then over my breakfast food and his sandwich and all the unspoken improbabilities of the two of us finding ourselves in this funny 50's diner laughing together like we really have a reason to be here. And I wonder if we look to the waitress like a couple, if she thinks this is one of those montages like I thought it was supposed to be.

I don't pay attention to the time, and we're almost late leaving for the church thing on the other side of town. Maybe that's the time warp cliché, that I lost track of the hours I spent talking to Casey even if I can't remember exactly what we said. Maybe we didn't really say anything.

He pauses with his hand on my door as I climb up into his truck. "You're sure you want to go?" he asks.

"If you do," I tell him.

"Okay," he says, and walks around the hood. When he pulls out of the diner's parking lot, he hands me his phone. "Kaitlen texted," he says.

I try to give the phone back. When he doesn't reach to take it, I set it in the cup holder where he had it plugged in.

"You can read it," he says. "It's about a game they're playing tonight. It'll be late when they're done."

I tell him I can leave whenever he needs to go home, but he says it doesn't matter, that the Everfelds are okay with him staying out.

"You have a game tomorrow, though?" I ask when

we're stopped at the light across from the Dairy Queen on Fifteenth.

He looks at me. "You'll come?" he asks. "With Bimi?"

"Okay," I say, and then we're both smiling when the light turns green.

I guess it's that I'm happy, that I'm finally relaxed—maybe not relaxed, exactly. Jittery, I guess, excited—when we're sitting in the church eating the cupcakes Toni Larkins' mom made with our little plastic cups of Coke.

So I don't see it coming. My mind's on other things, on how close Casey is to me, on our knees almost touching in the pew. Not on Kaitlen leaning in to whisper in his other ear. Not on Chad Frederickson answering all of Pastor Dave's questions in the front row. Not on Sophie Matton on my other side, secretly checking her phone in her pocket and then looking back at me and Casey and trying to get Kaitlen's attention across our bodies.

My mind's not on the sermon, either, if that's what it is. Because of course Pastor Dave's said these things before, about coincidences, about synchronicities that aren't right. That are evil, even. He hasn't shut up about them over lunch all week.

"It can be numbers," he says when I finally look up at

him. He's looking back at me, ignoring Chad's hand waving, ignoring the dinging of Sophie's phone out right in front of her face now.

"Maybe you think it's a coincidence. Maybe you see the same number in a few different places, and you don't know it's someone from the other side—some*thing*—trying to send you a message. Trying to control you."

It's just that I haven't broken eye contact, I tell myself. That's why he hasn't looked away.

"Or maybe it's dreams," he says. His voice is quieter now, but he's still looking at me. "Maybe they start coming true."

Afterwards, when the others are grouping up in the lobby for what Kaitlen's pitched as a sexier but simultaneously more holy version of ghost in the moonlight, Casey catches up to me before I can flee into the restroom.

He asks me if I want to go, because he must see this on my face, and I tell him I do. I almost tell him why, even, right there under the clock in the church lobby I'm afraid to look at even though I know it's at least an hour past 7:20 and nowhere near 2:05.

I don't look at the clock on his dash, either, as we pull out of the parking lot. Neither of us talk, and I stare out my window as he drives us back to the park.

The lights in the lot with my car are already off—the park's supposed to be closed after dark—and I can only see the line of trees that catch Casey's headlights as he pulls into the side entrance.

I'm out and a few paces ahead of him when I hear something. Then he grabs me.

It happens too quickly, the breeze from the car speeding past and how quickly Casey pulls me out of its way. We stumble into the woods.

My back's against a tree now. I haven't caught my breath. His arms are around me as the rumble gets quieter, the car pulling back out onto the main road. Then the blood rushing through my head is all I can hear for a while.

He's asking whether I'm all right when I can focus on his voice again. The car must have swerved at the last minute. Or Casey did. I felt it brush by me; it would have hit me if he hadn't gotten there first.

I don't move, and neither does he. I'm looking at him now, into his face that's just a shadow and the sparkle from his eyes when they catch some light from nowhere. Because he's Casey Everfeld, and this feels so right, whatever dreams and numbers brought me here to him.

He lets go of me but doesn't step back. I can feel the space between our bodies then, can feel my heart and swear

I can feel his, too, beating in the air between us.

And this can't be evil, I know, whatever Pastor Dave was saying about the forces that might have brought us here. Because Casey couldn't be that. So if it's evil that got us to this point, it must be in me.

9

Casey

I'm in the zone by the middle of Sunday's game at Lincoln, and I pitch three strikes in a row in the fifth. I guess that's what it is, the zone people are always talking about. I don't hear the crowd anymore, don't hear whatever Greene's yelling or any of the other guys. I lost track of Aarons, our catcher, a while ago. It's like I don't need him to know what to throw anymore.

Instead, my mind's on Mischa sitting between Rick and Ellen in the bleachers over the dugout. She smiles at me when I run back after the last strike.

It takes me a second as I put on the sleeve Coach has ready for my arm to process what he's saying. It's my confidence, he thinks, that's making this game. I guess he thinks I didn't have enough of it before. Not like this, anyway. Greene's pretty sure my fastest pitch was when he wasn't clocking me last practice, but I think I've been this strong since Tuesday, since Mischa agreed to go out with me. So maybe he's right about it being a confidence thing.

He talks about state between batters, and I guess he thinks this is what I can't stop smiling about.

10

Mischa

I wake up from another umbrella dream a little after three on Monday morning, but this time, my sheet's soaked through with sweat—stress sweat, my mom would probably call it—and my heart's pounding in my ears. Like I was almost hit by a car again, not like I was just sitting out in the rain. It doesn't make sense that stress sweat could be brought on by just an umbrella, though, by a faceless person and an old memory.

I think about all the other moments that could have stuck in my subconscious. There are so many more important ones. But I guess my mom would say this is stress, too, having dreams that don't make sense, that they're just another sign I'm in too many AP classes this quarter. Because she always thinks I need to do less, that another flare's right around the corner, even if this doesn't feel anything like lupus.

When I close my eyes again, I think of Casey, and then dreams of him come easy. They make me sleep through the second snooze cycle of my alarm, a string of bells that fit into my dream walking around a garden with him somewhere I haven't seen before with wind chimes clanging around in the breeze.

He stays on my mind as I get ready. But maybe he's supposed to be on my mind now that we're dating or whatever it is we're doing. Hanging out? Talking? I should have paid more attention to Rick's guesses, to the words I'm supposed to know.

As I drive to school, I ruminate on all the possible variations of 'dating.' Then I start hearing his name as soon as I get through the double doors in the pool hallway. I feel a flush creeping over my cheeks each time that I hope just looks like a butterfly rash, but it feels warmer, more noticeable.

It's because of yesterday's game, I guess, but it seems like everyone else is thinking about Casey Everfeld today, too—the group of freshmen clogging up the Science and Tech hall. Bimi and Nate. Mr. Warner when he congratulates the team in the morning announcements at the beginning of Econ, and then I feel Kaitlen Miller's eyes boring what I'm sure she'd say are very occulty holes into the back of my head through the rest of the class.

I keep hearing Casey's name everywhere as the day goes on. But I don't notice it anymore when I'm with him at lunch, and then we walk to Thesis together and talk quietly in Mrs. Stevens' room until the bell rings like Kaitlen isn't shooting her Satany death rays back at me.

Thesis flies by, and I'm not really paying attention to Kaitlen's presentation until she gets tripped up during the question period. Mrs. Stevens is trying to convince her the witches in "Macbeth" weren't being controlled by evil forces, that they were more *foretelling* witches and a bit of comic relief in a tragedy than, you know, *possessed* witches. Kaitlen's convinced they were something else, though, something darker, a vehicle for some greater force. *Vehicular* witches, I guess you'd say.

I can barely see her ponytail's shaking. Her glare's moved from Mrs. Stevens back to me, like somehow I might have done something to the "Macbeth" witches.

"But then how'd they know what was gonna happen at the end of the book?" Kaitlen demands. "They had to be getting that information from *somewhere*."

I look at the clock—Because I'm not afraid of clocks, I remind myself, and I know it's nowhere near 2:05—and then back at Casey. He smiles.

I try to smile back, try to ignore Kaitlen's witchy demands and the word 'occult' being repeated over and over as she answers all the other questions she doesn't have answers to.

Because today, at least, isn't for thinking about the occult or about dreams or numbers. So I focus on my notebook again, doodling in the margin and thinking about Casey, instead.

Out in the woods on my log after school, I keep hearing Casey's name from the baseball diamond. It's too loud; I've never been able to make out names from this distance before. I have to restart the outline for my thesis three times before I really get going with it.

It's at least an easy comparison between Gilman's story and Poe's. Gilman's narrator thinks she's going crazy when she's not, when her husband's gaslighting her, whereas Poe's narrator is convinced he's not crazy at all and is trying to convince the reader of it even though he's a murderer. It should be so easy to write these differences, but it's Casey's name that keeps getting in my way.

It's not until baseball practice is over that I finally get something reasonably coherent out of the outline and decide this is enough for today. Outlines must be one of those distractions my mom's worried about, the way boys are supposed to be, even if none of the other boys I ever went out with or talked to or did anything else with affected me like Casey Everfeld does.

So I try relaxing like she's always suggesting, putting my work in my bag and lying back on the log with my e-reader I've just downloaded a fun novel to. It's not exactly meditating, but I imagine I'm currently the inspirational poster for 'Chill' lying here in the shade reading a satire. And maybe I do relax some; I'm actually laughing out loud when I hear a branch crack.

I sit up and see Casey's face right away. He smiles, and then my smile comes easily, too.

He doesn't make much noise as he ducks under the branches. He's wearing the team sweats and a fresh white tshirt, his hair still wet from his shower. "I didn't mean to interrupt your book," he says when he gets to me.

I scoot over on the log, but he doesn't sit down.

"Good practice?" I ask.

He nods. I'd think of this as an okay quiet between us then, a comfortable silence, if he weren't still standing. I put my reader back in my bag.

"They must be really excited for you," I say, "after the game." Mr. Warner said yesterday was some sort of record for him.

"Yeah," he says, then, "thanks for coming."

I scoot over some more. It feels weird looking up at him like this.

He runs a hand through his hair and looks away, and some part of my brain registers this as a cue for something bad. As a breakup indicator, maybe, like it would be in a movie. Am I about to be dumped? If we were dating, I mean. It's likely I'm not even dumpable at this point.

I shift on the log. Maybe I should be running away now, I think. Suddenly, it feels like I should be running.

"I don't have to go to prom," Casey says once I've played through a few dumping scenarios in my head.

"What?"

"I don't have to go to prom," he repeats.

I wait. Not because I'm waiting for him to say something else, but because I have no idea how to respond to this.

"I mean if you don't want to," he says.

I start to say something—*prom, want to, me*. But none of these words come out.

He finally sits down, and now that he's at my eye level, I can't look at him anymore. I fiddle with the zipper of my backpack, the sun hot on my shoulders like his gaze is hot on the side of my face. I swear I can feel it.

"Go with me," he says.

And then it feels like the heat's a part of me when I look at him.

"I do," I manage after a second, "want to." I almost tell him how much. And maybe I would if I could, if this feeling were something different, something I'd had before and understood better.

He smiles and looks down at the log, at the space between his hand and mine.

"You're sure?" I ask. "You're sure you don't want to go with..." I don't finish this. I don't want to. There are so many other girls Casey Everfeld should be going to prom with; I'm about the three hundredth most likely, by my calculation, and that's just in our school. But I don't want to think about this list now.

"I want to go with you," he says.

And as I sit with him in the fading afternoon sun, I savor this. I don't think about whether it's real, about whether I'm being pranked or whether there's something manipulating him or me or both of us. I only know what this feels like now and how if I close the little gap between our hands, if I just touch his pinky with mine, I won't doubt anything else, either.

So I do, and we stay this way, our pinkies linked, until the sun's slanting low and orange through the clouds.

11

Casey

Tuesday, things are different. I don't know how it could feel like so much has changed in a week—not even a week since I asked out Mischa in the atrium. It shouldn't be long enough to change anything, but it is. Even baseball's different. These early mornings in the locker room after workouts are different. *I'm* different. For the first time, I feel like I'm exactly where I'm supposed to be.

It's like coming off a high, Aarons says as we're getting out of the showers, but he means the blowout Sunday. There was a scout from the league there watching me.

I almost say it's not the game, if the guys can see something's different about me now, that baseball's not everything.

But Justin Miller does it for me. He's already changed

and is hanging around the bench waiting for the others when I get out of the shower. "Heard you got a girlfriend," he says when I pass by him to throw my workout uniform in the laundry.

He has his lips pursed in that pissed off way Kaitlen always does. I guess it's genetic. Justin's a freshman and not even a relief pitcher yet, with Perkins behind me. So as far as baseball goes, he should stay pissed off for a good while.

"That true?" Enwell asks as some of the guys in the other bay come over.

"She was at the game," Miller adds, looking at me. They all are now. Kaitlen must have seen us in the woods and guessed.

I laugh. I can't help it. Because maybe Kaitlen's *prescient*, the word she used in Thesis yesterday over and over talking about her paper about prescients. Or witches. Or vehicles. Or whatever they are.

But I am *ecstatic*, I tell the others, not with that word— Mischa's word, just once when she was answering a question about some group reading. Not about me or about prom, but I know now that this is what I want, to have Mischa feeling as ecstatic about me as I am about her.

And the other guys must see it, too, must hear it in my

voice even though they're all still high on Sunday's game and itching for the double header with Madison this weekend. Aarons whistles. Perkins slaps my back. Miller at least has the sense to keep his mouth shut.

I hurry out of the locker room, wanting to get to Mischa before the bell. She and Bimi and all that group wait in the pool hallway in the mornings. I'm thinking about her when I'm jogging past the mechanical room and almost slam into Pastor Dave.

I apologize and try to keep walking, but he stops me.

"I didn't get to talk to you on Saturday," he says. "You left before the others."

I look at the stairs and say something about the bell. I guess I'm not a very good convert or whatever.

He starts walking with me, but too slow. "I'm glad to catch you," he says when we hit the landing. "I wanted to talk to you."

He's a couple steps behind me, and I almost trip when I turn back to him. "I don't go to church much," I tell him when it seems like he's expecting me to say something.

"Not about that."

"Okay," I say. And I guess this shouldn't be creepy. I think it's just the way he is. Maybe it's a youth pastor thing, but the last one wasn't this bad, was he? And he only came to lunches.

"I just wanted you to know I'm here if you ever need to

talk," he says.

I stop then. Dave does, too. Because I don't know why I would need to talk to a pastor. Do I look lost? I couldn't look lost now, I think; this is the first time I've ever felt *not* lost. I tug down the zipper of my pullover. I'm too hot from the shower.

"Anything you need," Dave says, clapping me on the shoulder like Greene does. "Just know I'm here. I'm on your side."

I thank him before I take the stairs two at a time and get to Mischa just before the bell.

12

Mischa

Before I meet Bimi and Nate and the others Tuesday morning, I feel a burst of energy like I could power through a dozen first period Econ lectures. I don't know if it's left over from yesterday in the woods or if I slept better last night or if I dreamed more or dreamed less, but my head feels clear, finally, when the cooler air hits me at the pool hallway.

Nate mirrors Bimi's mouth-locking gesture, and they can't stop smiling when I get to them. They know about prom already and have questions for me as soon as we're a few steps away from the others—how Casey asked me and how we'll do pictures and dinner and all the other parts of the night that don't really matter to me. I still hear Casey's name louder than everything else whenever it comes up—

Everfeld, Everfeld, Everfeld, everywhere.

He gets to me just before the bell rings and walks with me to my locker, and I'm still smiling when I hear his name behind me in Econ, souring in Kaitlen Miller's mouth.

By the time I'm in Bio, I swear the Kaitlens are multiplying. They all have the same lines, too, at least that I hear, suggesting Casey asking me to prom is some sort of a joke. There's a Serena now (not very serene) lingering around my locker during passing periods and another cheerleader Kaitlen calls her Ali Bear (more appropriately named, very much like a bear) who seems to be everywhere.

It's like the Kaitlen clones all just noticed me at once, like I popped into existence for the bigger players in the Centerville High School ecosystem at exactly eight o'clock this morning when it became widely known that Casey Everfeld asked me to prom.

"Mischa," Bimi says for the fourth time in the lunch line. Maybe I should be focusing more on what she's saying than on counting the times she has to get my attention.

I turn to look at her, but I can feel Kaitlen's glare from all the way across the cafeteria where the cheerleaders are selling cookies.

"You have to not let them get to you," Bimi says.

I tell her I'm not letting anyone get to me and even try to act like I haven't noticed all the talk and glares suddenly directed my way. This is just an adjustment, really, since I've never been the subject of any gossip before. I guess because I haven't dated a jock before, and the star one. Or maybe it's just something about Casey, whatever it is about him that makes people pay attention.

"This is *good*," Bimi says as we're running our cards at the end of the line. "You're happy. You and Casey are gonna be good together. I can see it on you."

My eyes land on some of the guys from the baseball team crowding around the table they've run together with ours. Crowding out Pastor Dave, I notice, who's over with some swimmers today a couple tables away.

The guys on the team—I can't remember all their names. Perkins, I know, is one of them, from Casey talking about him—greet me and Bimi as we sit down, and they tell me about Casey's class on the other side of the building, how he'll be here soon. They've left the seat next to mine open and taken the one he was sitting in before, across from me and one to the right.

I wait for them to say something else before he gets here, for the collective shock that Casey Everfeld is supposed to be sitting next to me, that he would ask someone like me to prom, but it doesn't come. His friends are just one mass of jockness at the far end of our table, but *polite* jockness trying to make conversation with the rest of our group as Bimi and Nate fall into their usual happy murmur.

Chris Perkins—he introduces himself again—points out Casey as soon as he walks into the cafeteria, in case I didn't notice, and I remember to eat my pizza.

While Casey's still in line, Nate offers to get my usual chocolate chip cookies from the cheerleaders' table, obviously aware of the Kaitlen evil eye, and I thank him. Then the rest of lunch period flies by in an easy haze.

After Thesis—a longer one, it seemed like, with Kaitlen in full form—I head for the parking lot, grateful that it's Tuesday and I can leave early. Not that the talk was getting to me. Or maybe it was, slowly. It's like hearing it drained my energy even though I felt so good when the day started. Maybe prom talk is like lupus.

Casey's quiet as he walks with me. He holds open the door at the other side of the atrium and follows me outside.

"I've got gym last," he says when I think he's going to go back. "Greene knows where I am. I don't have to hurry."

I nod, and as I suck in the humidity, it feels like everything inside fades away. Like this really is as good as it felt before.

The flags are whipping around over us in the breeze, and there are just a couple cars cruising through the intersection out on Fifth Street. I look back at the doors, and my notebook slides off my binder.

Casey grabs it before it can fall. "You're okay?" he asks as he tucks it under his elbow.

I tell him I'm fine. And I am, at least now that we're alone, now that I'm not hearing our names everywhere. I *should* be fine, anyway; the multiplying Kaitlen Millers of Centerville have never bothered me before.

"Can we talk?" he asks.

I nod and follow him to his truck, climbing in and watching as he walks around the hood and gets in the driver's seat. I try to think of what to say now, of how to sound okay. Okay like I know this is what I want, even if I didn't know I wanted it before. It's so clear to me now that this *is* what I want, though, being here with him with the doors shut and this feeling like nothing and no one outside of this truck matters. Even if I know this feeling won't last.

"Will you tell me what's going on?" he asks when he

closes his door. "Nate said the cheerleaders were being bitchy."

I take a breath and push on my stomach like I used to whenever something was going to come up that wasn't supposed to. Then I give Casey the light version of what I heard today, like all of it really did roll off me.

He curses when I mention people saying he only asked me to prom as a joke. I guess my laugh doesn't sound right, that I don't sound as unbothered as I'm saying I am.

"Who said that?" he asks.

I shrug. It could have been any of them. It could have been all of them. I think it probably *was* all of them, at some point, all the Kaitlen Miller clones I never noticed until this morning.

Casey runs a fist through his hair, spiking it up, then sets his hand on the armrest between our seats. "You don't believe that shit," he says.

I look at his palm. "No," I say, because right now, at least, I don't.

His fingers twitch. "The guys, they like you already, you know. We could walk with you during passing periods so nobody'd..."

I tell him I don't need anyone to walk with me. I have enough people worrying about me as it is, and it's not like I'm going to suddenly fall into a flare—or something worse, I guess, something emotional—just because another silly girl says my name in the wrong tone of voice or spreads a rumor about me and Casey that doesn't feel true when I'm with him.

He doesn't seem to let out any air until I set my hand on his, though.

"Thank you," he says, and I'm not sure if he means for my hand or for not believing the Kaitlens.

"I'm okay," I tell him. "Are you..." I don't know how to finish this. *Under the influence of some evil force*, I almost say, a la the occult, but instead, I laugh for real, because this sounds almost as ridiculous in my head as it does when Kaitlen says it.

Casey squeezes my hand. "You can ask me," he says. "Anything."

"You don't have to get back for gym?"

He shakes his head.

It takes me a minute watching him to get my breath steady, even, like his. "Are you sure this is what you want?" I finally ask, but I'm looking at his dashboard now.

He pulls my hand towards him as he twists to face me. "We don't have to go to prom," he says.

I can feel the warmth from his hand crawling up my elbow, my shoulder, across my chest. I pull mine away. But I can still feel something—maybe not heat, but *something*

—between us as I watch him put his hand back on the armrest, his palm up again, open.

"It's whatever you want," he says. "We could wait till next year or not go then, either. I don't care about prom."

I open my mouth at the "next year." It sounded so easy for him to say. He must not have been thinking about it. But isn't there some rule about when you join your lunch tables and walk to classes together and talk about next year? Maybe this is too fast. *Maybe this is witchcraft*, Kaitlen's voice in my head screeches.

"This can go whatever speed you want," Casey says, because maybe he can read my mind now. It would be him doing something to me, I think, not the other way around, if there were something otherworldly happening between us.

I look at him. Then my hand's back in his, because this isn't something I have to think about.

"*Is* it too fast?" he asks.

I shake my head, because I'm not sure what would come out of my mouth now. I think I'd admit it's something in me that's changing too quickly, that's making me dream about him and hear his name over and over. That's making it hard for me to focus on anything else. That's making *us* feel not fast, not new at all.

"If it's the others," he says, "if they're bothering you, we can stop them from talking. I'll walk with you and tell the guys…"

"No," I say, because I wasn't thinking of anyone else. Here in the truck with him, it's like every Kaitlen insecurity in my head, even every *me* insecurity in my head isn't there anymore.

"I thought you'd want to go with Nate and Bimi," he says, "but we don't have to."

I look up at his face. I guess I've been staring at his hand for a while.

"Prom," he prompts.

"Prom," I say. "Right. I want to go, I mean, if you do."

He smiles. "Okay," he says.

"Okay," I echo. And then I can't look away from his face, from his smile that's everything I need to see right now.

"If *I'm* ever what's bothering you…If I ever stress you," he says, "you just have to tell me. I want you to be sure."

"I know," I say, and I don't tell him exactly how sure I am.

I walk to the little park across the street to finish my homework on the swings, wanting to avoid any chance of running into Kaitlen, but once Casey's practice starts, I imagine I can hear baseball hits and even his name on the wind every now and then.

It's early when I run out of work—even Precalc goes fast—and when I get home, my mom spends dinner asking about my stress levels again.

I don't think about my mom or about stress again until later, when I'm just getting out of the shower and I hear her talking to my dad through their bedroom door.

I don't tune in until I hear the word 'distracted' a second time and realize they're talking about me, that she still thinks I'm getting distracted. By something. *From* something. I don't even know what this could be; school's going fine. And 'stressed,' the way she always says it. I've gotten so used to hearing that one that it sounds like her voice now whenever I say it in my head.

My dad's voice is calmer. It's harder to hear through the door, but at least it sounds like he disagrees with her. Mom's gets higher and higher before they both go quiet again.

Later, I tell myself whatever they're arguing about really isn't about me, that I'm one of those teenage scapegoats for middle-aged marital non-bliss and they just haven't had a chance to be non-blissy middle-ageds before now since their marriage has been solid. It can't be me, I think, because this isn't stress I'm feeling now. This is something else.

I set my phone on my nightstand and imagine I hear a subtle buzz of electricity before the chime of a text message comes through. I know it's Casey before I pick it up.

Good night? he asks.

Great, I tell him, and wonder how anyone could look at me now and think I'm stressed.

13

Casey

Wednesday, I swear the universe is conspiring to keep me away from Mischa. I get stuck in traffic on the way to school, and then Greene calls me into his office during lunch.

"You want coffee?" he asks as soon as he sees me in the door. So this is a serious talk. I look at his old stained mug next to his keyboard.

I tell him I'm okay, and he asks me to close the door.

"You're all right, you're all right," Greene says. "Just don't want anybody to get their hackles up." He gestures for me to sit.

I pull off my backpack but stay standing.

"It's that scout I told you about from the league. He called yesterday. He'll be at Madison Saturday."

I say "okay" and then add a "that's great" for the team. But I'm kind of a done deal at State College, I remind him. Their coach has been talking to me for the last two seasons. State, barely half an hour from The Artsy Fartsy, as Greene calls it, Mischa's school. Or at least her first choice. And she'll get into her first choice, I know. She's already aced the SAT. She doesn't even have to retake it next year.

"You've got time," Greene says.

"Sure. But I still like State." And the league scout's only seen a couple flukes. I was never throwing like that before.

Greene picks up a pen and starts tapping it on the side of his desk like he does with his clipboard in the dugout. "State's good," he says, "but that was before. You weren't like...there wasn't anything like these last couple games to make you rethink college ball. To think you might be moving on to something bigger right away."

I almost tell him I don't *want* something bigger, but I stop myself in time. Because baseball's what I've always been focused on, what I thought I wanted before.

"I just want to make sure you're thinkin' about it," Greene says. "That's all. I know it's lots a pressure. Lots a pressure," he repeats, frowning at me.

And maybe he's right. Maybe that's what I feel all through my body now, pressure. Too much, like I could explode. Not at Greene, though. Greene's always had my back. And not over this. This isn't something I should feel pressure about. This is something I should feel good about.

"The scout's not gonna wig you out this weekend," Greene says, asking like he isn't the one sitting there trying to wig me out right now.

I tell him I won't get wigged out, and he finally lets me go in time to grab a slice of pizza to eat on my way to Thesis.

It's raining, so Mischa heads straight home from school when I go to practice. I text her after dinner, and she tells me she's fine, but I can tell something isn't right. It's her parents being weird, she says when I push, but I know the girls are still getting to her, too. They won't say any of it around me, of course. Nate had to tell me everything he'd heard.

I can't stop thinking about it when I go to bed. Maybe that's why I dream all the shit I do, because I almost never go to bed angry. I don't even know how many dreams I have or what happens in each one—nothing's clear, and I'm just angry each time I wake up. Angry and worried about Mischa.

When I wake up the last time, my phone says it's just quarter past five—I don't know why I check my phone. I know she won't text me in the middle of the night—and I get ready to go for a run while it's still cool out to clear my head.

I'm surprised when Rick runs into me at the front door.

"You're up?" I ask, because he's usually half dead until he's working on his second cup of coffee at the dealership around ten.

"Couldn't sleep," he says. "You, either?"

"Guess not."

He sighs. "I'll put on coffee. We can talk."

"Better not be a serious talk," I joke as I follow him to the kitchen.

He laughs as he gets out a couple mugs. The blue light on Ellen's coffee machine's on, but it's not gurgling yet. I guess it's too early for the timer.

"Greene?" Rick asks.

"Who else?"

"Well, you knew it was comin' after Sunday's game." He joins me at the table when the machine starts to grumble. "You're a star and all that. You okay with all the pressure?"

Pressure again. "Sure," I say, because I don't have anything *to* be but okay or excited. And I think I'm more okay about this. Not about Mischa. About Mischa, I'm definitely excited. And terrified.

Rick reads my mind. "How's Mischa?" he asks.

"Good," I say before I admit I'm not really sure. I know *I'm* good with us, at least, and that's what I want to think she is, too. Better than good, like I am. But I don't deal with all the girl drama at school.

Rick nods. "Nate told me," he says. "He said Bimi was pretty pissed off about it. But Mischa's okay? I mean, she still wants to go to prom with you?"

"She says so."

"Good," he says. "Smart girl."

I check my phone again. Nothing. But she could still be asleep. She *should* still be asleep.

"Maybe you'd better have her over here instead of going out this weekend," Rick says. "Nate'll have Bimi Friday, I bet. Wouldn't Mischa be more comfortable with that, so you wouldn't run into any of the other girls?"

My head jerks up. I should have thought of this. "Right," I say, and even with Rick watching me, I can't help but smile like a lunatic as I text her.

14

Mischa

Thursday morning, I sleep through the second cycle of my alarm dreaming about a freaky room I don't recognize. It's a tiny, bright space, but it feels big somehow, like something big's coming. My sheets are sweaty again when I finally sit up.

The dreams before this one were all running. But that's probably something about the last quarter of the school year and taking too many classes, isn't it? I'm sure that's what my mom would say, that this is classic stress.

My head goes back to the room when I close my eyes, and then it takes me a minute to climb out of bed and get to my phone. When I unplug it from the dresser, I see Casey's text.

Tomorrow night, it says, *hang out here with Nate and Bimi? Or something else?*

I sit down at my desk. It's that rush I'm not used to, a rush I didn't think I could get from something like a text message. Maybe this is what being a teenager's supposed to feel like. Or it's a psychological trick because Casey uses punctuation and spells out words like 'something,' and this is a novel experience for me with boys. But I know it's more than spelling that makes me flush in that not-about-to-throw-up-from-sun-poisoning way. This flush is good.

School feels better today, too, like the talking's settled down some now that Casey and I are older news. I guess this really is a teenage thing, how some days can feel like years and this thing between us feels stronger than it should be only a week and a half since he apparently noticed my existence.

At lunch, Bimi and Nate chatter about movies for tomorrow night at the Everfelds. Casey and I learn we like the same genres—quiet stories, light stories. Not like Bimi and her period dramas or Nate and his thrillers.

My thesis is coming along well; I got a draft of about half of it last night when I ran out of *The Handmaid's Tale* to read. And Kaitlen faces forward today in class, sulking. I look at Casey, wondering if he's said something to her, but he just shrugs and smiles.

Serena's disappeared during passing periods since Chris Perkins started talking to me by our lockers, and Ali Bear seems to have moved on, too. So when I come out of Precalc at the end of the day, I guess I'm not expecting anything bad. I head down the pool hallway to go out the side door.

It's seeing Pastor Dave's face, not his saying my name, that stops me. I don't remember seeing him at lunch today, but I guess I wasn't paying attention to any of the other tables.

I start to say hello and blow by him, but then he's walking with me and holding open the door to the lot. Maybe they have another teen thing this weekend at the church and he's recruiting. That's what they do, isn't it, recruiting?

But he doesn't say anything about church. "I wanted to talk to you," he says as I take bigger steps towards my car. Not towards the woods. Casey's practice will go late tonight. They don't have one on Friday, and the away games Saturday are a big deal, so this will be a long day for him.

I try not to look towards the stadium as Dave and I cross the drive in front of Leena Thompkins, Bimi's lab partner in Mr. Menkin's Chem class. I wave a thanks at her.

"Actually," Dave says when we're a few steps into the lot, "I thought *you'd* want to talk to *me*."

I stop a couple cars down from mine. "Talk to you?" I ask.

"I know what's going on with you," he says.

My breath catches. I hold it as I turn away and dig through my purse for my keys. Because my breath shouldn't catch now. This isn't *The Handmaid's Tale*; religion isn't scary.

"I don't know what you mean," I say when I've finally let this air out.

"You can trust me," Dave says. "You can talk to me about what's happening."

I try to look at him, but my heart's too fast, and I'm dizzy. It's the sun, I want to say, and something about lupus. But I know this isn't lupus. So I swallow and tell him that I'm fine, just busy with a lot of classes—that's what my mom's been saying is stressing me. She's probably said it in one of those chat rooms for parents and that's where he got it.

I throw a "thank you" over my shoulder as I jog the rest of the way to my car, but Dave's still standing there when I pull away.

As I pass the intersecction, I stare at the bumper of the car in front of mine and try not to look at my dashboard clock.

I guess that's why I'm so restless through the night. Not because I haven't talked about it—*them*, all the dreams I've had and the number that seems to keep coming up and the weird room with the shimmering walls I see twice tonight and the way Casey Everfeld is suddenly interested in me. Because I know, whatever I still *don't* know, that talking about it won't help.

Or maybe I don't want help. Even if all of this, if what brought me and Casey together came from some sort of a lie or a trick, I know already that I'd be willing to lose so many other truths to hold onto it.

I'm awake, my heart racing after the room dream when my alarm finally goes off Friday morning. I think I'm going to throw up at first, and I sit still and take my pulse, health class-style, for a few minutes before I stand. The dreams were fuzzy this time, no baseball maneuvers or memories of umbrellas. Those were happy. These were all running again, other than the room. I feel like something important will happen there soon.

The nausea passes after a few minutes, and as I'm getting ready for school, I tell myself these are just nightmares, things I can leave behind me. Not prophetic like the baseball dream. I even tell myself that maybe I really am just stressed, like Mom says again over breakfast when she can see my concealer doesn't quite cover the bags under my eyes.

I tell her I'm fine, that I was up late working on my thesis—because I'm excited, because at least that feeling's true, consistent, just about going to Casey's tonight rather than about Poe and Gilman and madness.

When I get to the pool hallway, Casey's already there talking to Bimi and Nate. He sees me right away, and when I get to him, I'm struck by how seamlessly he's integrated into my life in this short time we've known each other. My friends have started talking with the baseball guys at our table, and Casey's even won over Kirsten with softball talk. Nate's gotten into a routine of picking up my cookies so I don't have to face Kaitlen, since Casey's always a little late getting to the line. It feels like we've been doing this for a while.

It's almost *too* easy, I tell Nate when I thank him at lunch, joking that I'll get spoiled by cookie delivery and Kaitlen will only hate me more for it. But I don't really care about Kaitlen Miller or about anything that's too easy, too *right* in my life right now.

"So it's okay if I pick you up at six?" Casey asks as

we're walking to Thesis.

"I thought I was coming at seven."

He grabs the door to Mrs. Stevens' room. "To meet your parents," he says.

I tell him he doesn't have to pick me up at all—I can drive—but he says he wants to.

The day's easy energy propels me through my presentation I'd almost forgotten about and the question period after that earns big Mrs. Stevens smiles and the go-ahead for moving forward with the rest of my paper.

Later, I rush out after an early dismissal from Precalc, wanting a chance to wash my hair and find something to wear before Casey comes over. I don't see the figure by my car until I'm already across the lane.

Pastor Dave doesn't turn around until I get close, and it doesn't hit me as a surprise, exactly, when he does. Even though I wanted it to be someone just hanging out in the parking lot waiting on the traffic. But there isn't any traffic yet.

"I need to talk to you," Dave says when I get to him.

I look behind me. Nobody else in this row's out yet, and the lane's quiet. There's only the rumble of a few cars pulling out of the senior lot behind us.

"I need to get home," I tell him, trying to make my

voice come out strong. Not scared. Because I shouldn't be scared of this man, of words. And that's all he can do to me, really, say something I don't want to hear.

Dave's still standing in front of my driver's side door when I come around.

"Excuse me," I say.

He shifts but doesn't get out of the way. I take a step back before I can stop myself and look over at the atrium doors. Casey should be out soon. I should have waited for him. I shouldn't have said I was in a hurry to get home.

"I know what's going on with you," Dave says.

I square my shoulders and take a breath. "I don't know what you're talking about," I tell him. My voice cracks this time.

He reaches for my arm then, and I stumble back into the hood of the next car.

His hand drops. "I'm not going to hurt you," he says. "I just want to talk to you. To help you."

I can feel my heart now and the sun on my arms. I try to slow my breath, to straighten up and look certain when I tell him I don't need his help.

He takes a step towards me before glancing over his shoulder. The car at the end of the line's pulling out now, but away from us. No one's driving this way.

"You *do* need my help," he says, then, "This isn't fair

to Casey."

And I don't know why that's what does it, why I can't get enough air all of a sudden at just his name, at this quiet implication that came from a stranger, someone who doesn't know me at all, someone who couldn't know my dreams or anything else that's happening to me.

I try to tell him to go, to leave me alone, but it's Casey who's there then, Casey who grabs Dave's arm and shoves him away from me. Dave's hip slams into my back bumper.

I don't hear what they're saying. I can only hear my body, and then I'm sitting on the asphalt and there are people stopping by to see what's going on. I look out at all the shoes. Only shoes, I tell myself, like I used to when I needed to sit down. Not people looking at me.

"I'm fine," I say when I get my breath. "I just had a..." Was it a panic attack? "There wasn't anything..."

There wasn't anything. There wasn't. There wasn't anything that happened, wasn't anything Dave said that was inappropriate that put me here having to catch my breath on the asphalt. So I get up and steady my legs under me, trying not to make eye contact.

Casey opens my driver's door, and I sit. Maybe I need to again.

Bimi and Nate are in front of the hood now, and Casey closes the door and says something to Nate. Bimi glances at me a couple times while Casey's talking to them, then turns the shade of Bimi red I've only seen one other time, when Adam Mountjoy smushed a cricket she'd found during recess in second grade and she shoved his head into the triangle bars so hard it got stuck and he didn't get out until Mrs. Zimmer came to find him when he didn't come back inside for class.

I should get out of this car now, I know, should tell Bimi I'm okay. Because I'm not a cricket. But then she's in the passenger seat.

"That shithead," she says as soon as she's slammed her door closed. "Are you okay? What did he..."

"He just wanted to talk to me."

"That *shithead*," she repeats, and then something about harassment, how Nate's parents will call the school and tell them what happened, how Dave won't be allowed back on campus.

"I'm fine," I say again. "It was just...I don't know." Because I *don't* really know, do I, what he was going to say? Maybe it's just what anyone could see, that a Casey Everfeld does not belong with a Mischa Kenning-Elliott. That these things do not go together. Like the puzzles in the kids' magazine I used to read with my mom, *Some Things Do Not Belong.* Not that something's happening to me— the occult, or whatever Dave would call it, what he's always preaching about at lunches to feed Kaitlen's boob heaves—and that's why Casey's with me.

"What did he say to you?" Bimi demands.

"Nothing."

Bimi shifts and looks at me for a minute. "Okay," she says, "so you don't have to tell me. But you're gonna go home with Casey, and Nate and I'll meet you there later. I'm texting your mom and telling her you're with me."

I start to say she doesn't have to do this, even start to tell her I wanted to wash my hair and wear a new top tonight, but she's looking at my hands. I do, too, then. They're shaking.

"It was just a panic attack," I repeat, steadying my fingers on the steering wheel.

"Okay," she says, "but that shithead's still not coming back here, you're still letting Casey drive you to his place, and I'm still texting your mom.

The cars around mine are all gone, and the line out to Fifth Street's backed up when Bimi finally gets out, promising to bring some makeup and those facial towelettes she uses to the Everfelds' tonight. I'm pretty sure Bimi could face an apocalypse with just what's in her purse and am almost disappointed that I don't wear fuchsia lip gloss.

Casey opens my door, and he doesn't say anything as

we walk to his truck. When I hear something behind me, I spin around and almost fall.

The sun, I say right away, that it's just getting to me since I was out in it more than I'm used to. Because it's Casey who's behind me, not Dave. And definitely not anything that should make me spin around so fast I lose my feet.

Casey's stopped. "I scared you," he says.

"No." But I can feel my heart thumping in my stomach now. I twist my hands, trying to stop them from shaking.

"I'm sorry," he says.

"It wasn't you. It was…" I want to say it was something else, something that *really* wasn't him, that wasn't related to him at all. "It was just that he surprised me. And the sun."

Casey doesn't come any closer.

"It's okay," I tell him. "He just freaked me out, and I was already...it was a panic attack." I say I'm better now, whatever that means.

"You'll come with me?" he asks.

I tell him of course I will and repeat that I'm fine, letting him open the door to his truck for me to climb in.

15

Casey

I think Mischa's still shaking, but maybe it's me.

She smiles from her bar stool, trying to show me that she's all right, as Rick microwaves some samosas for her. That's what he thought was important right now, samosas. They're emergency samosas, obviously nut-free for Mischa. I must have read the label five times after he told me he was sure. Ellen's in her office talking to somebody on the school board about the pastor.

Overstepping, Rick called it. He thought Dave must have just *overstepped* when Nate called and gave him a heads up about what happened in the lot. You know youth pastors, Rick said when Mischa was in the bathroom.

No, I told him, I *don't* know youth pastors. Neither should the Everfelds, I think now. *Us*. I'm supposed to think of myself as one of them. But the only *us* I feel tonight is me and Mischa. It's like everybody else is a threat, like everybody else could be. Even Rick, who's trying to help.

"Casey?"

My head jerks back to him. I don't know what he was saying to her, only that she seemed okay a minute ago, eating some pretzels out of a bowl Ellen left out for her.

"Yeah," I say, hoping this is the right response. Because I'm trying to take it easy like he said. So I wouldn't make Mischa any more stressed out than she was already.

Rick raises his eyebrows at me. "So Ellen and I'll pick up Mischa's car on the way back from our movie," he says.

Mischa tries to tell him she'll get it tomorrow, but he says this is "easy peasy," and she eventually gives in. She's looking at me now.

"Easy peasy," I repeat, trying to keep my voice *easy peasy* as I walk over and take the bar stool next to hers. I grab a pretzel, but chewing hurts. I don't know what I've been doing with my jaw. Clenching it, I guess, like I used to when I was pitching. My whole face hurts now.

"You're feeling okay?" I ask her at the same time she asks if I am.

"Fine," she says.

"Good," I say, and take too long to swallow the pretzel.

16

Mischa

I forget about the parking lot as the night goes on. Like I didn't have to be driven here, like I wasn't just having a panic attack in the middle of the freaking junior lot from something as stupid as a pushy youth pastor trying to counsel me. Because that's all it was, really, an attempt at counseling me. And isn't that what youth pastors are supposed to do?

I only have to not to think about what he was trying to council me *against*, about whatever he thinks is wrong with me—whatever he *knows* is wrong with me—with respect to how it affects Casey. But what Dave said was so vague, it almost gets lost in my hand in Casey's as we sit on the sofa together watching some drama I'm not really paying attention to while Bimi and Nate snuggle in one of the big armchairs closer to the TV.

The Everfelds are back from their movie already and upstairs. They left out extra samosas and pretzels for me, more than I could possibly eat after the big Mexican dinner Rick cooked.

When the movie's over, Bimi and Nate go up to his room, leaving me alone with Casey.

He gets up to get the remote, then switches off the TV. I can't see his face for a minute as my eyes adjust to the darkness. My hand's cold when he leaves it.

I think at first that he's going to ask me about Dave, to try to get me to talk about it, so I guess I'm more anxious than I should be when he asks if I want to go outside, instead.

I agree, but it takes me a second to stand up and follow him. To the kitchen. To the side door off the laundry. Every step feels slow tonight, and I think so many times on our way there that I'll say something, or that he will, and it won't be what I want.

But Casey doesn't say anything. A breeze comes in when he flips the deadbolt and opens the side door. The wind hits me harder outside then, a little gust that's not really cold, but it makes me shiver anyway. Tonight's humid, and I feel the moisture creeping over my arms and goosebumps popping up as I walk towards the fence separating the Everfelds' yard from their neighbors'.

I stumble over a tree root, and Casey catches my elbow. "You're cold?" he asks, looking at my arm.

"No." And I should be all out of shivers today. Tonight. It feels so different from today.

I keep walking, finding my way along the fence after leaving the puddle of light that's coming through the kitchen window. I stop when I get to a wood bench—not a bench, I realize when I'm close to it, a tree swing. I sit. I guess I still need to sit down.

Casey follows me, but he doesn't fill in the quiet like I want him to. I can only make out his outline silhouetted against the light when he stops a few feet from me.

"Talk to me," he says when I think I'm about to say something—anything.

So I do. I say the first thing that pops into my head, leaning back and looking up at the sky. "I can't see stars." Because it's clear tonight; we should be able to see stars.

"It's the streetlights," he says.

"Are you going to sit?" Maybe this thing has made me braver, feeling so wimpy earlier, being so affected by something that wasn't anything, really. Maybe I'm compensating now.

He sits down, and the seat rocks back before he catches it with the toe of his shoe. My side sways forward a little, then settles, stills. He's still, too.

And maybe that's why something comes out of me when I don't want it to, when I should be saying something simple, like about the weather, instead, if I trust myself to say anything at all. Weather talk would count as eloquence for me tonight.

"You don't have to go out with me," is what I say. "I don't want you to feel like you..."

The swing jerks forward when his toe lets go. He reaches out a hand to catch my back, then wraps it around my waist to hold me like I really am going to fall like I feel like I might now.

He curses, but it doesn't sound like him. Then he apologizes, drops his arm, takes a breath. "That's what Dave said to you, something about me? Like what the girls..."

"No." But I guess I'm not convincing. Casey's breath hissses out. I twist to look at him, but his face isn't catching any light even now that my eyes have adjusted to the darkness.

"Whatever it was..." His voice softens then, goes quieter. "Whatever he said to you, I'd feel better if you'd tell me."

So I do, kind of. And I tell myself it's enough for him to know I'm feeling guilty about going to prom with him, that it's enough that he thinks it's because of the other girls, about what they're saying, that I really *have* told him what I'm afraid of. Not of Pastor Dave, exactly. Because I can honestly say I'm not scared of Pastor Dave; he only scares me when I think about him and Casey in the same breath, about whether this could be fake, induced somehow, this thing between us. Because it's real to me.

There's a while of quiet after I'm finished. There should be crickets, I think as I look back up at the sky, still waiting for Casey to say something. There should be something other than quiet now.

Finally, I feel his pinkie brush against mine on the wooden seat. His palm's up again, an invitation. So I set my hand in his, and he wraps his fingers around mine.

"If there's something I can do," he says, "so you won't worry about whatever anybody's saying..."

I shake my head. "I'm not worried about them," I say.

He picks up my hand and sets it on his chest. "Is this what you want?" he asks, but he keeps going before I can tell him this is *all* I want, that he's all I can think about right now, all I can focus on. All I want to focus on.

"This can be whatever you want," he says. "Is *this* what you want, right now?"

"Yes. This," I say, softer this time. "Now." I want to think much longer, to tell him this thing we have is all I'll *ever* want this much, because I feel like I know it already.

He keeps my hand at his chest. He's already turned

towards me on the swing. I'm facing him now, too, my right toe brushing the dirt under us.

When you kiss someone like this for the first time, they say that the stars line up or that planets collide. That sparks fly. That the ground shifts under you.

But that's not what this is. This isn't something outside of us, isn't an electrical thing or something happening light years away in the sky.

This is something in me and in Casey, between my body and his. In the warmth as he turns my wrist to press my palm flat against his chest. In his breath on my cheek as he leans in. In how I feel like the stars and the skies and whole universe are between our lips right now.

I thought that time would speed up, but it feels like it's slowed down, instead, when our lips collide like planets don't. I can't tell the difference between our breaths then, between me and him and everything outside of us, or at least what used to be outside of us, and at least for now, nothing beyond us matters.

17

Casey

At the second game at Madison on Saturday, I almost forget where I am when Perkins runs back to the dugout. His hand slaps my shoulder when I don't reach out for it. Another run. That makes nineteen, I think. Maybe twenty. So now we're up by...however many it is. A lot.

I used to always know, used to watch the game and plan the next inning in my head, pitch by pitch. But my mind isn't in this now. My mind's on Mischa, just her and this feeling there's something wrong with her. Even though I don't have a reason to think anything's wrong. It's just the look on her face, the way I'm imagining it in my head when I shouldn't be imagining Mischa at all.

One of the guys gets a hit—Who was up? I don't even know how many outs there've been—and I don't see Greene next to me until he says something.

"Looks like you've got some jitters," he says.

I start to tell him I don't have jitters, that I wouldn't get *jitters* after pitching a near perfect game all the way up to whatever inning this is. Late. The last one, maybe. But I say something about my head, instead, and this is what he latches on to.

"You've got a headache?"

"I don't know," I say, because now that I think about my head, it actually does hurt. But I know this isn't a normal headache; this is something else, something that's never happened to me before. Fear, maybe. It feels like fear, but it's about something I don't even know to be afraid of. So maybe I really do have the jitters, just not about the game like Greene thinks.

I think he'll yell, that he'll tell me to get my head in the game, but he puts a hand on my shoulder, instead. "Your eyes look a little glassy," he says. "You could be comin' down with something."

"It's just my head," I tell him. Because that's all it is, what I keep seeing in my head when I'm not focused on something right in front of me. It's making it harder and harder to focus on anything else.

Greene grunts. "Lots a pressure," he says, like he does. "Lots a pressure. Let's call it a day for you, then." He waves a hand at the stands, at the scout who's been watching. He's seen all he needs to. Why risk it, and all that, if I'm not at my best for the end of the game, Greene says.

"Give Perkins a chance to pitch the rest," I agree.

Greene looks at me for a second, then nods.

I go to sit down, but he gestures to the end of the dugout. "Get home and rest," he says. "I'll tell 'em it's migraines."

I don't know if he sees something's wrong on my face or if I really look that bad now. I didn't feel this way earlier. It didn't hit until my last few pitches.

"No sense ruinin' a good thing," he says when I don't move right away. "And we need you rested and ready for next weekend."

I thank him and almost trip over my own feet as I grab my bag and run from the dugout.

In the car, I text Mischa twice in a row, with a *Hey* and then an *Everything okay?* when I don't think I can wait any longer for her to write back. We're only at Madison's town square when I check my phone again. There's nothing.

Ellen's twisted around in her seat. "Something wrong?" she asks.

"No."

"You don't look good."

"A headache," I tell her again.

Ellen looks at Rick. He glances at me in the rearview. "Let him be," he says. "Good to let Perkins pitch for the scout, too. And you pitch that good of a game, you deserve a break."

I meet his eyes in the mirror and try to smile like this is it, like this could be about baseball.

"I'm not tired," I say when Ellen suggests I get some rest.

She frowns at me. "Your head..."

"It's better."

She goes quiet then. They haven't turned on the radio or anything. I look out the window. We're not even at the junction to Franklin yet. I know this line of towns from the last two seasons. Madison's never felt so far away from home before.

I almost jump out of my seat when my phone buzzes. Ellen turns around. I ignore her, fumbling with the phone as I click on Mischa's text.

Can I come over to talk?

Of course, I say right away. I wait for the little dots to tell me she's typing again, but they don't come. She reads it as soon as it's sent, though.

We'll be another hour, I tell her. *Are you okay?*

Fine.

But she *isn't* fine. I don't know how I know it or why I'm so sure I do. "Can Mischa come over?" I ask when it's been another minute—or maybe not that long. Maybe it just feels long—and she hasn't said anything else.

"Of course," Rick says at the same time Ellen says, "It'll be so late."

"But it's a Saturday," Rick finishes for her, and then they're both quiet the rest of the too-long drive home.

After I tell her we're back, Mischa texts to say she'll leave in a few minutes. I look down at my sweats. Maybe I should have put on jeans, taken a shower. She won't be here yet. I have time.

But something keeps me at the windows of the den. Jitters, I guess. When Ellen asks me what's wrong, I tell her I'm fine, that I just need to move. So I pace around the kitchen and in the hallway where Mischa and I went out last night.

"I'm leaving," I yell behind me before I know I've decided this. But I have to go. I'm sure.

"What?" Ellen asks. "Are you picking her up?"

But I'm already outside, and I don't bother to answer as the door snaps shut behind me.

18

Mischa

Saturday night at dinner, I must look stressed. Both of my parents are watching me as I push a piece of cauliflower around in a puddle of melted butter on my plate.

"It's all your classes," Mom says. "You're distracted."

I don't bother asking her what I could be distracted from, if it's not classes. Isn't that what I'm supposed to be focusing on, school? I'm not distracted from school, obviously, not distracted from college applications I'll start next fall—I already know where I want to go—not distracted from any of the things that parents and teachers are always saying teenagers get distracted from, like this is what we do, just get distracted, and that's what throws our lives so off track.

"Classes are fine," I tell my mom, and say again that

I'm not tired. They want so badly for me to be tired.

"Mischa," she says, the way only she can say it. She's shaking her head now. "You're spreading yourself too thin."

I set down my fork. "I'm not stressed," I repeat, and it sounds like all the other times I've said it. I've been trying different inflections lately, but they're all starting to blend together. "I'm...bored," I try, in case this is better somehow. Maybe bored looks enough like tired. And I almost do feel bored with school.

Mom looks at Dad with that look she makes when she's not buying something. Like I can't see it, like I'm not here.

Because I'm *not* here, I guess; I really am distracted, just not how she thinks. This isn't about my grades or junior thesis or college or whatever else she thinks it could be. This isn't even the kind of high school relationship drama she expects. This is my phone that's in my purse on the chair in the living room and all the things I haven't said to Casey that I should have. All the things I need to say.

I try to tell myself it's a matter of communication, that it's just that I don't know *how* to say these things, like this could be about what words I pick and not about what I'm actually telling him. Words I have trouble just saying in my head. Because there are things I haven't come to terms with yet, like that I knew the score of today's game before it came on the radio in my dad's office and that I've seen 7,205 at least twice in the last day. That there's really something happening to me, something I can't control. Something that's controlling *me*. And probably him, too. Because Casey Everfeld never asked me out, never even noticed my existence before these things started.

But that sounds batshit. *I am batshit now*, my head reminds me, like this is just my new normal, another baseline I'll get used to. My mom may as well be saying it, too. And my dad, even though he's so chill usually. He's very *not* chill now as he watches me from across the table.

I don't know what they think is going to happen; I've never said anything about shooting up a school or anything, even joking. My grades haven't slipped at all. I haven't joined a biker gang like in that book we had to read in sixth grade. So you'd think they'd chalk this up to teenagehood and let me eat.

I take this opportunity to remind them I'm a teenager. Not batshit. There has to be some distinction. I tell them I was thinking about prom, like Mom's brought up twice tonight. That's the ticket, prom. It's something I could be stuck on and be totally normal. I say I'm worried about my new dress that's the same as Kaitlen Miller's and wonder why I didn't think of this before. *Silly Mischa, be a teenager*, my head sing-songs in the voice from that commercial, like it wasn't sounding crazy enough before.

"You know you don't have to go," Mom says. "I'm sure Casey could find somebody else who'd..."

"*Lisa*," Dad says.

"*Stan*," she returns. They're both holding their forks over their Saturday steaks. Because we're saying names now. This is what dinner conversation's come to.

"*Mischa*," I say, pointing to my chest as I stand and pick up my plate, leaving the table.

In my room, I rehearse what I need to say to Casey. I try to think about the truth first, about anything at all I can tell him that's true. *I tricked you?* But that's not right. *Someone else...* I think of Pastor Dave's words. *Something else is bringing us together. Something that's my fault, not yours.* Because maybe I haven't been trying to get rid of it, exactly; it's not like I've been making an effort to stop these dreams and feelings and just knowing things I shouldn't. I wanted to see him this afternoon, wanted to know how the game was going. And that's when I saw him in my head, when I knew how much they were winning by and how well he was pitching.

So it's me wanting this connection to him. Intent, like we kept going over in Intro to Law class last semester. Mr. Lahr must have said it a hundred times, repeated what it meant like we might actually mistake it one day. It seemed so simple in the book. Maybe I should be writing my junior thesis on intent instead of on madness.

I squeeze the phone in my hand and reread my last chat with Casey. It feels like so long ago. I go back to the text box, trying out a few things before I eventually land on, *Can I come over to talk?* and send it before I can rationalize my way out of this.

Of course, he writes back right away. The game must be over already.

I sit on my bed and try again to find the right words. I want to think there's an easy lie I can offer, since I don't like the truth. I'd rather say I'm *not* taking advantage of him, not keeping secrets from him. When I remember Dave's words about how this isn't fair to Casey, whatever I'm doing to him, I want to scream that it isn't fair to me, either. It isn't fair that I feel like this. It isn't fair that I should have to give up this relationship just because I got lucky in some way I'm not supposed to. It's like I won the lottery but the store cheated, and now I have to give everything back.

It's okay, that voice in my head keeps interrupting whenever I start to form these lines, *you're not doing anything wrong.* Because this is the voice I want to hear— mine, I think, but it's not like I'm able to tell the difference anymore. Maybe I should have taken Psych last semester instead of Law.

My phone lights up on my nightstand.

We'll be another hour, Casey says. *Are you okay?*

Fine, I tell him, and then I repeat it to myself over and over, picking up my phone to check the time every few minutes until I can leave.

My mom's in the kitchen when I come downstairs.

"You're dressed," she says.

I glance at my arms, at the old half zip I pulled on from my hamper. I'm glad I grabbed something dumpy. It guess it fits how I'm feeling. And there's no reason to try to look good when I'm telling my boyfriend he's *not* really my boyfriend, that this isn't what he wants and hasn't been his choice from the beginning. It's not like any makeup would have held up.

"I'm going out for a ride," I tell Mom, and this isn't a lie. I hope biking over will at least give me a chance to exhaust myself first. These night rides used to clear my head. The Everfelds' place isn't that far, and the streets are all quiet this time of night. And maybe when I get home, my mom will think the redness on my face is from the wind stinging my cheeks like it used to riding in circles around the neighborhood when I couldn't get to sleep.

"It's cool tonight," Mom says, then, "Do you want to

talk?"

I shake my head and tell her again that I'm not stressed. This has become a habit. The ride's just exercise, I say. I need to get out. I've been studying so much.

She nods. She won't check my phone through the family account or anything. She's not that kind of mother. Or I'm not that kind of daughter. I wasn't, at least, before.

And I'm feeling guilty for that, too, when I get to Wilson Street, just a block from Casey's house. The wind's in my hair, making a rumbling in my ears as it rushes by. But at least it dries the tears before they can make it out of my eyes.

I feel like I haven't had to pedal for a while, like the Everfelds' place is all downhill from mine and I'm being pulled towards Casey somehow.

I take my feet off the pedals and actually have to start braking when I get to his street. I almost get out my phone to call home and tell my parents where I am. But then there's a louder rumble, and everything goes dark.

19

Casey

Sometimes I think she squeezes my hand. I count her breaths. I was halfway to the truck when I started. An ambulance would have taken too long, they said when we finally got to the emergency room. Before surgery. Before they sent a social worker to me. *For* me. Because this was *harrowing,* the surgeon said. Because she had no fucking idea.

But Mischa was breathing. *In. Out.* That's what matters. All that matters. They were wrong about her spine, the surgeon said. I had to listen outside the room then, when her parents came. I tell myself they'll be wrong about her brain, too.

A nurse comes in with an IV bag and tells me again that Mischa won't wake up tonight. I can't keep track of which IV this is or if I've seen this nurse before. There are so many of them here with the beeping machines and the bags on shiny metal poles and all the tubes that hold the patients together, tying them up in plastic knots until their bodies can heal and stay together on their own.

I squeeze Mischa's hand and tell her I'm here.

Her parents have the other side of her. That's how we've split her tonight, down the middle. They pat her arm sometimes but otherwise don't touch her.

I don't listen to the questions her dad asks the nurse this time. There hasn't been any new information for a while. Now we're just waiting.

Mischa's lucky, they said. Lucky I found her. Lucky I could carry her and her bleeding brain. Lucky the way her head twisted when it hit the pavement wasn't just a quarter of an inch more, where her skull collapsed in on itself. Lucky her spine wasn't...what they thought when I carried her inside. I'm supposed to be grateful now, they think, just that she's breathing. *In. Out.*

"Deal with after, after," her dad says to her mom when the nurse leaves. *Stan.* Stan and Lisa. They keep telling me.

Lisa nods. She hasn't said anything for a while. Maybe they gave her something like they tried to give me. I thought she'd be screaming when she saw Mischa like this. Everything in me was, but Lisa wasn't here to see the blood. There's a bandage wrapped all the way around

Mischa's head now like a turban. To keep everything stable, the surgeon said, like she might fall apart without it.

"You should eat something," Lisa says, to me this time. "You've been..."

"I'm fine."

"We could call you in the morning," Stan offers. That's how he introduced himself, as just Stan, when he shook my hand in the hallway when Mischa was in surgery. I still had her blood all over me then.

"No," I tell him. "I won't leave." There are only supposed to be two people in in this room at a time, but they made an exception for now.

"It's like you were sent here to protect her tonight," Stan says after a few more breaths.

I don't say anything. Because I should have been there before the car hit her. I could have caught them, could have stopped them. I could have been holding her on the sofa now, not squeezing her hand while she lies on a hospital bed wrapped in tubes.

In. Out.

20

Mischa

I dream of Casey. Not playing ball this time, but here with me. I know he's close even though everything's dark and I don't know where *here* is.

But this is okay, I want to tell him. *I'm* okay. I try saying it a few times, wanting him to hear, to understand, to know this as well as I do.

I fall back asleep still saying it.

21

Casey

Sunday, everything's the same. I watch Mischa's breaths and now the little lines on her heart monitor, too, listening for the beeps. I don't know where all the other lines coming off her body go to, but I count them sometimes waiting for something to change, for her to twitch or for her eyelids to move. Anything.

But there won't be anything, her doctors keep telling me. At least not while they're keeping her under, while they're giving her all these drugs. They say I should get some rest.

I keep having to tell everybody I don't feel like resting; if anything, I'm *less* tired today. I can hear more, too, all the doctors and nurses moving around in the hallway, the elevator doors opening and closing, the typing at the computers, the chairs rolling around the nurse's station.

I jump, and my hand jerks—but it's mine, not Mischa's —when the doors across the hall snap shut. "I'm sorry," I tell Mischa.

Lisa and Stan don't look up this time, him in the armchair, her lying on the cot they brought in last night. I guess they're used to me talking to Mischa now. Because maybe she can hear me, one of the nurses said earlier, when they were down in the cafeteria getting breakfast. She said I should keep talking to her. Rachel, her name was. She's on my side, showing me Mischa's chart whenever she can.

Rachel's with the surgeon when she comes back in. It's almost shift change, and they'll say I have to go this time— there's no exception for second nights, since Mischa's stable now. 'Stable' is what they call it when they're keeping her asleep and don't know anything about how she'll wake up. About if she'll wake up.

But they only check who's in the room at the beginnings and ends of shifts, Rachel told me earlier, when I was ready to fight with them all, when I felt like that was what I had to do to stay. So I only really have to leave twice for about an hour each time.

Rick's waiting for me at the elevators when I make myself go. Because I shouldn't be driving, he said this morning when he came to take the truck home, like I was the one hit.

As we walk down to his car, he asks me the same questions he and Ellen have been texting all day that I haven't responded to, about Mischa's spine and about what the doctors are saying, about how she looks and how her parents are holding up and if there's anything they can do. But there's still nothing any of us can do.

I'm just getting out of the shower—it's only nine, my phone says. I'll have to wait another half hour to go back—when I hear the yelling.

I run down the hall, pulling a towel around my hips as I go. There's something wrong. There has to be; Rick and Ellen never yell, never fight. They're not like any of my foster parents before.

They're quiet when I get to their door.

"Casey?" Rick asks after a second. He must hear my breathing.

"You okay?" I ask.

"Fine," he says.

They're waiting for me to leave. So I go back to my room and hurry getting dressed.

They'll be quieter now, more careful. They'll go downstairs to Ellen's office. It's almost soundproof when the doors are shut. Almost. They don't know my closet vent's right over her computer. I guess those are the kinds of things you don't think about with guest rooms, at least when you don't plan on adopting anybody.

I wouldn't normally listen, wouldn't normally lock my door and throw a bunch of shoes out of the way in the closet, trying not to stomp around. But this isn't normal. None of it is.

I'm already lying across the carpet when the door closes behind them downstairs.

At first, all I can hear are murmurs, not anything clear, and I tell myself I shouldn't be doing this. I've never spied on them before.

"Things can change," Rick says, loud now.

I freeze. I've just gotten my hand under the grate to lift it up and put my head down in the vent.

Ellen says something back, softer. I set the grate on a pile of dirty t-shirts and hit my head on the edge of the vent. I freeze, thinking they've heard me, but then there are murmurs again.

"You should have told me." This time it's clear. Ellen. Angry.

"I didn't know," Rick says.

I hold my breath. I almost imagine I can hear beeping inside my body then, too, my heart letting me know it's still going like Mischa's is.

Ellen's pacing. I can hear her steps. Rick must be standing still.

I only catch a few words. She's talking too fast. *Plan. Casey. Him.*

Him.

Then Rick, softer now. *Sides. Roles. Parts.* They're on a team, it sounds like. *Not my team*, my head says, and my head's hot now. All of me's hot. My leg twitches, kicking the hamper.

"We've got to stay out of the way," Rick says. He must yell it. Or maybe I can just hear better now, like I can hear every ping in the metal of the vent. Like I can hear the way my knee scrapes across the carpet and the sound my arms make as they shake, holding me here.

And then Ellen really is yelling. There's more to it, though. Her voice isn't right; she's crying. Ellen, who never cries.

"We don't have to know how it all plays out yet," Rick says. He must be standing right under the vent.

I only catch a mumble in response before the heat kicks on, blasting dust into my eyes.

When I can finally go back to the hospital, I take my time coming down the stairs. Rick's at the table and has a paper in his hands. It's the Sunday paper he always reads in the morning. He should be through it by now.

Ellen's making tea, but she hasn't put enough water in the kettle. It's doing that rocking thing when the bottom gets too hot. I can smell some cheese left over from last night smoking on that burner.

I want to yell at them. One of them. Both of them. I don't even know why.

But don't do it, my head tells me. My head's usually not this loud. Maybe that's why I listen to it this time.

Ellen turns around when I get to the bottom of the steps. "You're not going back already," she says. "Shouldn't you get some sleep for..."

"I'm not going to school tomorrow." It comes out hard, loud.

She flinches, then reaches for the towel on the oven handle like she's drying her hands. I think for a second she might fight me on this. "Let me get you a thermos," she says then, "so you'll have something to drink."

I watch as she pours iced tea from a pitcher in the fridge into one of her bottles. I can't keep my body still. It's like all of me's shaking now. I need to get out of here.

I squeeze the bottle when she hands it over, my hand heating up through the metal.

"You'll text how Mischa's doing?" Ellen asks. "We'll

be up."

I nod. I can't look at her.

Rick crosses the kitchen to get his keys.

"Don't," I tell him. "I need to drive." I try to hold still, to not show him I'm shaking.

Then he takes a step back. "Okay," he says, "if you're sure."

I get down the hall and to the side door, where I can almost feel the heat from outside—everything's hot now—before his voice stops me.

"You trust your instincts, son," he says. "You're right where you need to be."

I turn around. He's in the doorway to the kitchen, a shadow with the light behind him.

"I will," I tell him, and then I'm gone.

22

Mischa

I wake up to voices—fuzzy at first, but then clearer. A man's voice is the first thing I hear, one my dad calls "doctor."

This man repeats himself when my parents ask him the same questions over and over. He still doesn't have answers. But he will soon, he says. Because I'm so lucky. So much better than anyone could have expected me to be. Healing so well. Because we are *so lucky*. He must say it a dozen times.

The woman who comes in later, the surgeon, says the same things about luck. So my mom should sound better, I think, now that she knows what I do, what I could tell them if I could just talk.

But Mom's voice is far away, barely a whisper.

My dad's is better, stronger. "He saved her," he says.

Casey, I know right away. He means Casey. He could only mean Casey.

So I'm surprised when I can make out my mom crying. Not about me, surely. Not about good news.

"How do we know he's not..." She stops. There's some rustling around somewhere—another person coming in, doing something. I hear a creak, and then it's quiet for a while.

"He's got to be with us," my dad says when I think they're going to stay quiet.

"For now," Mom says. And that's it.

But it was serendipitous, the first doctor said. I want to remind them now. S-e-r-e-n-d-i-p-i-t-o-u-s. It's the word I won the fifth grade spelling be on. My mom didn't cry then.

It feels like more like *synchronous*, I think now, like all these synchronicities are what make me alive at this moment and not dead. The ones I thought were bad before, but maybe they're why I'm here, why Casey's coming back to me soon, when he'll have my hand again. I'll try to squeeze it this time, I think as I fall back asleep, to show him I really am all right.

23

Casey

By the time the sun's coming up Monday morning, Mischa's floor's busy. There are more doctors in today for regular hours, all of them saying things about physical therapy and the other things they think Mischa'll need when she wakes up. Not yet, they say. But at least they're talking about her waking up now.

They tell us it'll be slow going. They're going to start tapering her off the meds soon, since her last scan came back good, and then it'll be a couple more days before they can reevaluate things. They use a lot of words like that— They *think* things. They *reevaluate* things.

I don't have to look at Mischa's parents to know they're still freaked out. Like I am. Even though every doctor who's come in today has said how lucky she is.

Some nurses come to take her for another scan, and we're left alone together around the time they usually go to lunch.

"You're not going to school?" Lisa asks when I guess she feels like she has to say something to me.

I tell her I'm caught up. I don't tell her I had perfect attendance until this morning. So I have a lot of days I can stay here without Rick and Ellen or anybody else trying to stop me.

Stan pats me on the shoulder like Greene does. "You holding up okay?" he asks.

I nod and remind them about the Everfelds' offer to bring by food or look in on their house while they're here. But they don't have pets waiting or plants dying or anything. They only have Mischa.

We sit in the quiet until the nurses wheel her back in.

It's not long after Stan and Lisa leave to get dinner that Ellen comes by with another sandwich. She waits for me in the room across from the elevators since this floor doesn't let visitors clog up the halls.

I thank her when I get there and take the bag. It's a reuben from Frank's like they used to take me out for after games, when we had something to celebrate.

I try to think of this as celebrating, too. Because Mischa's made progress, the doctors keep saying. So that's what I tell Ellen, that at least things are going better than they expected. But I stop when I really look at her face.

"What is it?" I ask.

"Nothing." She turns away, looking at the vending machine like she's going to get something. But we both know she wouldn't eat anything in there.

"What is it?" I ask again, setting the sandwich bag on the table.

Ellen gestures to the sofa in the middle of the room. I follow her there but don't sit down.

"How are you feeling?" she asks once she's on the middle cushion.

"Fine."

"You're not worried about Mischa?"

"Of course I'm worried about Mischa." I start again on what the doctors have been saying like she might not have heard me the first time. I guess this is what I have to think about now, how Mischa's going to wake up and be okay, be *her* again. I won't get through this if I think anything else.

"How are *you* feeling?" Ellen asks again.

I look at the door. An older man passes by on his way to the elevators. He's the one who visits the guy in the room next to Mischa's. I've been gone from there too long.

"I don't know what you want me to say," I tell Ellen. "I'm fine."

She nods but doesn't get up.

"Can I go?" I ask, grabbing the sandwich bag. "I want…"

"Were you driving?"

"What?"

She's still not looking at me. "Did you take the truck, when you found Mischa? Were you driving?"

"No."

"Then how…" She stops.

I look at the wall she's staring at. There's just the vending machine there.

"How'd you get her to the hospital?" she asks.

"I carried her to the truck. Like I told you before."

"Then you…you couldn't have hit her?"

The bag with the sandwich falls out of my hand. "What?"

A nurse pokes her head in the doorway. My voice must have been loud. But Ellen still hasn't answered.

I take a breath and try to keep my voice lower this time. "Why are you asking me this?"

Ellen shakes her head. "I'm sorry," she says. "I didn't

mean..."

But I don't wait to find out what she didn't mean. I leave Ellen where she is and go back to Mischa.

It's Dave I find, though, on his way into her room.

Sometime later, I'm standing in an empty room down the hall. The veins on my arms are all popped up, blue. The head nurse is here with Rachel and a guy from security. Mischa's parents are standing behind them. They're all looking at me.

"He didn't hit him or anything," Rachel says in my defense.

I keep my mouth shut. *I should have hit him.* I only grabbed him, but I wish I would have hit him. I could have. I could have done a lot worse.

"I don't understand," the other nurse says.

I haven't been able to say anything yet. I swallow and try to slow my heart. My knees are starting to pulse now. I think it's from standing still. I need to move. To chase him down. To stop him from ever getting near her again. I could.

I take a breath, then another. But it's like I have *too* much oxygen now. When I think I can keep my voice steady, I tell them as clearly as I can what happened Friday in the junior lot.

"What?" Lisa asks.

I get my phone out of my pocket and hand it to her. "The numbers for Rick and Ellen are in there," I say. "They can tell you. Ellen called somebody on the school board about it. Dave's not allowed back on campus."

"It was a...a panic attack, you said?" Rachel asks.

I swallow. "That's what she said."

Mischa's mom looks at my phone in her hand, but she doesn't scroll through the contacts. "This was Friday?" she asks after a second.

"Yes."

"That's why Bimi texted me after school?"

I nod.

She hands back my phone. The head nurse and the security guard look at each other.

"Okay," he says then. "We'll put in a note. He won't be allowed back on this floor."

I want to say this *is* okay. I should thank them, at least, for not doing something to ban me, too. But I just nod, because I don't think gratitude is what would come out of me now.

24

Mischa

My parents are talking about Pastor Dave again. They keep asking Casey what happened Friday like they don't believe him.

I've been telling myself to wake up for a while now. Finally, I feel my eyes open. There's pain, and I can feel my head, suddenly, and my back.

It's Casey my eyes go to first, though, Casey whose hand I feel in mine, and then none of the other feelings matter.

At the beginning, it's hard to talk. My throat's scratchy, but I don't have to say much, with the doctor who comes in right away and the nurses trying to prop me up against the pillows and everyone talking at once.

This doctor's surprised. They didn't think I'd wake up yet, he tells me, and he keeps saying things about how I'll need to rest like I haven't been resting for—however long it's been. What did he say? Three days?

It's not very long before another doctor's here, too, this one a voice I recognize from before, the surgeon. She has me move my eyes in different directions and asks me to say some tongue twisters, wriggle my toes and my fingers and remember my teachers and my cousins like I could be a different person now in this body.

She doesn't say anything else about what happened. None of them do. 'Hit' was all I got, and 'accident.' 'Lucky' was what they said the most.

I look at my parents while she repeats all these things. None of them matter now. I try to tell them this, to convince them I'm fine, but they all just keep talking.

They don't want to stress me, the surgeon repeats.

"The pastor," I say, when I finally have a chance to, like I might not know my parents have been saying Dave's name over and over when I've been out. Like Casey's. "The youth pastor at that church. Dave Parker. He...I had a panic attack Friday after school." Because that's what I said it was, didn't I, a panic attack? And it's not my memory that's the problem.

My mom puts a hand on my hair and coos at me in the same voice she uses on her rhododendrons when she's overwatered them. She tells me not to worry, that they've already taken care of this, that Dave won't be anywhere near me again, that it doesn't matter now. That nothing matters but my getting better.

Casey squeezes my hand, and I tell them all—honestly—that I'm not worried.

25

Casey

I skip school again on Tuesday. When I have to leave the hospital at six, since visiting hours end earlier on Mischa's new floor, I drive straight to the police station.

The officer across from me now is looking at his computer. He hasn't typed anything for a while. "She said she didn't recognize the driver," hes says when he finally looks at me again.

I turn towards the hallway. I haven't been in here since our field trip in seventh grade right after I moved. Nobody's come by in a while. This officer was the only one I could talk to, the one whose name I can't remember. And this is all any of them do, it seems like, talk. What they're calling an investigation into Mischa's hit and run is over unless something new turns up, he told me; they're at a dead end.

"You don't have cameras at the lights or..."

He shakes his head. "A dark car," he says. "I'm sorry, but that's all she remembered, and there are a lot of dark cars."

I put my hands against the table. I can't stop moving them.

"You still say you didn't see it?" he asks.

Still. So he thinks I'm lying. But as soon as I got outside Saturday night, all I saw was Mischa. I'd have seen the car if I'd gotten there just a minute earlier. I should have gotten there a minute earlier.

"Probably a panicked driver," the officer continues when I don't say anything. "Happens more often than you'd think. Probably somebody young, maybe around your age, who didn't even see what they hit and kept going because they were scared."

"No," I say. "They were trying to hit her." For the second time, I think now. But I told them that already, about what happened at the park.

He looks between me and the computer screen. "I know this is stressful for you," he says.

"No."

He clicks on something on the screen, and it goes dark. "I know you said..."

"Dave Parker."

He nods. "We're looking into that, too. I'm sorry your girlfriend had a panic attack, but if there's not…"

I get up and leave before he can give me the same shit again.

When I get home, Rick has two mugs of coffee out on the table next to his paper. He's sitting down and seems to think I will, too.

"Maybe it's because they have a different lead," he says when I tell him about the station. "Maybe they can't say anything yet, so they're just not telling you what they know."

I don't say anything.

He gestures to the chair across from him and pushes a coffee closer to it, like maybe if I can smell it, I'll sit down. "This has been a lot on you," he says. "But you said she's doing well?"

I pull out the chair. It's loud as it scrapes against the tile. I almost knock it over. I did that at the hospital with the chair by Mischa's bed this morning. I don't know why I'm so clumsy now. So maybe it's good that I haven't tried to throw anything since Saturday's game. Or maybe I should have thrown something. Maybe then they would have taken this seriously.

"Mischa's doing good?" Rick prompts.

I tell him she's fine, or as fine as she can be with somebody trying to kill her.

Rick looks at the stairs, then back at me. Nate's up in his room with Bimi. "Nate thought she might get out soon, but that can't be right, can it?"

"That's what they say." Because she's so ahead of schedule, her doctors keep telling us. So they'll discharge her, let her go home so Dave can get at her again, right after he put her in there.

"That's good news, isn't it, for..."

"It's bullshit."

Rick opens his mouth, then picks up his coffee. "You don't think she's well enough?"

"*She's* not the problem."

"But she's healing, Bimi said, like...really well."

Healing. They keep saying that. And how it's a process, how now that she's stable, they'll watch her for another day or two on the new floor and then let her keep healing at home. Because homes are supposed to be healing.

"I'm sure her parents'll be extra careful," Rick says, "and I bet she won't be on a bike again for a while."

I pick up the mug in front of me, needing something to do with my hands. The ceramic burns my palms as I squeeze the sides.

"So she still doesn't remember anything?" Rick asks when I've just been staring at the coffee for a while. "The car, I mean, or anything else?"

"She remembers it was a dark color and something in the window, but that's it."

"Something in the window?"

"She can't remember. I should have seen him, if I'd left..."

Rick stops this with, "She's lucky you got there when you did. How Bimi tells it, anyway. I'm sure her parents are singing your praises."

I think of Mischa's parents as we sit in the quiet. By the time I remember Ellen coming to the hospital yesterday, the mug's cooler against my hands. Or maybe they've just burned, gotten used to the heat.

"Ellen asked me if I hit her," I say.

Rick sets his coffee down. Some splashes out on the table. "What?" he asks.

"She asked me if I was driving when I found her."

Rick looks at the stairs. "You weren't," he says, then, after a beat, "were you?"

I try to meet his eyes. He's using his sleeve to wipe up the coffee now.

"You told us you carried her," he says before I can answer. "That's what happened, isn't it, that you were running when you found her, and you carried her back here to the truck?"

"That's what happened."

"I believe you," he says.

"I didn't hurt her."

He looks at me, and I think he's going to tell me he knows this, that he knows I would *never* hurt Mischa, that I'd never hurt anyone. But he doesn't.

Maybe because he sees this isn't true anymore. I think of my bat in the hall closet. I can bat. Not as well as I can pitch, but well enough.

Maybe Rick's thinking the same thing, about Dave. "Don't go there, son," he says.

"Where?" But my hands are gripping my mug so hard now that it's shaking, the coffee sloshing up around the rim.

"I know what you're thinking," he says.

"You don't know shit."

Rick sits back, eyes me like he didn't think that would have come out of me. I guess I wouldn't have expected it to either, before.

"I understand how you're feeling," he tries.

"No," I tell him. "You don't."

He shrugs. "You're right. I don't. But I *do* trust your instincts. I know you'll do the right thing."

"I..." I stop. I'm hot all over now. Like I was when I saw her, when I started running. Like I know it's going to happen again.

Rick stands and comes over. I think he's about to put a hand on my shoulder, but he steps away when he sees my face. "This is a long game," he says then. "I think you know that. Sometimes there are bigger gains, bigger reasons when we don't get what we want right away."

My hands fist on the sides of the chair. He must see how much I want to kill Dave. How I could right now. I think of Mischa in the parking lot that first night at the park, then of Mischa over my lap in the truck blowing through the light out on Third Avenue, the steering wheel slippery with her blood.

"We've all got to play our parts right now," Rick says. "And I know you, Casey. You'll do the right thing."

26

Mischa

I was out of the woods, they said on Wednesday, and then yesterday, I was out of the hospital. So I thought I'd be allowed go back to school like usual this morning instead of taking a half day. Less than a half day. My mom took forever just to agree to drive me in, because apparently my parents think I can't be trusted to drive myself anymore, like what I had was some sort of a driving accident. By the time we finally pull up to the front entrance, it's after twelve.

She says something about the steps, about driving me around to the gym, before I jump out and swat the passenger door shut behind me, yelling a "thanks" over my shoulder. I take the stairs at a run then. It feels good to run, even through the heat in the middle of the day. It's like I have more energy, not less, like they keep saying I will.

Maybe I've *over*-rested with all the forced sleeping. Or maybe it's the drugs they gave me. They could tamp down the lupus or something, change my baseline. Maybe I'm the person who's accidentally discovered a medically-induced, lupus-curing coma. Today, I feel like I might really be this lucky.

I bounce on the balls of my feet while I wait for the office to buzz me in, and then I have to make myself slow down on my way to the cafeteria. It's like this isn't just lunch, isn't just a half day of school. It feels like there's something more important I'm rushing towards.

I look around the alcove, but I'm not looking for Dave anymore. My eyes land on Casey through the crowd.

He gets to me by the bathrooms and takes my book. It's just Precalc today with some notes for my thesis tucked in between the pages. I'm not allowed to carry a backpack yet because of the stitches on my shoulder. They're worried they might break open again, that *I* might break again, like I didn't have to be hit by a car first. But everyone's always assumed I was fragile, so at least I'm used to this.

A path seems to clear ahead of us as we walk to our table. Bimi's already gotten my pizza, and Nate's laid out cookies—extra today—on my tray. I thank them and tell everyone I'm okay when they ask. None of them say anything about the accident. They must have made some sort of pact before I got here. Instead, they say how pretty my top is and update me on all the gossip I've missed.

Mitch pauses a rant about Kaitlen's newest student council project—something with religion, of course—when I reach back to redo my ponytail.

"You look so good," Bimi says when everyone's been quiet for a second. "Like nothing happened."

I pull my ponytail around. But I'm getting used to it; I almost forget sometimes there's a chunk of hair missing at the back of my head. I thought it would be worse, but the ponytail hides it pretty well.

"We can talk about it," I tell them. "I'm okay."

And that opens the floodgates. By the end of lunch, I've given an account of everything I remember—or at least of everything I remember when I was awake, which was just the bike ride and then a couple days in the hospital eating a ton of jello. My friends ask what I can eat now, like maybe my cookie appetite's going to go all of a sudden, if I can drive, and whether I'll be able to go to prom. That one comes from Perkins. Because prom's only eight days away. Casey tenses, and Perkins starts to apologize.

"Of course," I interrupt, and then I tell them all again how okay I am.

But it's obvious they don't believe me. Bimi and Nate take a detour from their usual route to walk with me and

Casey to Thesis, and then after, Casey stays with me, flanked by Perkins and one of the other guys on the team, on the way to Precalc. When it's over, he's waiting for me at the door to walk me back to Mrs. Stevens' class since she asked me to stop by when I could.

"You should be at practice," I say when I almost bump into him as I come through the doorway.

"'s okay," he says. "Greene knows." But he's looking around this time, over my shoulder at everyone filing towards the doors to the parking lot. There's no one in the hall ahead of us.

"Dave's not here," I say, then, "I really am all right."

Casey's head snaps back to me. "Right," he says.

He waits just outside the door when we get to Mrs. Stevens' room, and she goes through the same *how am I feeling's* I have a script for now—*fine, healthy, almost no different than before.*

She gestures for me to sit down. "I just want to make sure you're dealing with the stress all right," she says. "And you know there's no reason to worry about your thesis right now." She gives me that sympathetic look she always has, the look every teacher has, really, since I got the lupus diagnosis in fourth grade. Like I *am* lupus, a conglomeration of all the things I can't do. I know how this goes. Next, she'll tell me how well I'm doing in spite of it.

Now in spite of being hit, too, in spite of the concussion, in spite of the stress of recovery.

"I'm almost done with my draft," I tell her, shaking off this newest set of *in spite of's*. I gesture to the hall, where Casey has my notes in my Precalc book. Casey never looks at me like this, never says anything I am *in spite of.*

Mrs. Stevens shakes her head. "No, no," she says. "Don't worry about that. You have plenty of time. You were so ahead when you got started. Don't let it add to your stress right now."

At least I know how to respond to this, after so many months of my mom talking about stress. After so many years, really, of them all saying the same things. I promise Mrs. Stevens I won't stress, that I'll get the draft to her on my own time. But I want to tell her the truth, that I have *more* energy now, if anything, and I'm feeling ready for what comes next.

Dinner at home's more of the same. I think this is at least normal, considering the circumstances, until I ask if Casey can come over tomorrow. He doesn't have any games this weekend, and my parents should jump at my not having to drive anywhere.

Mom's turned away now, doing the dishes. "I think you

should think about this," she says, but her voice sounds like she's narrating one of those documentaries about the gazelle who doesn't know the dry season's coming. Or that there's a crocodile in the river who's going to eat her after the commercial break.

"Think about what?" I ask. "Or I can go over there. The Everfelds are..."

"I mean Casey. You should think about Casey."

My dad looks up from his phone as I process what Mom said.

"Casey?" I ask.

"You've been spending so much time together," she says. "For the last week, he's been..."

"I was *asleep* for half of that," I remind her. I don't remind her he saved my life. I shouldn't have to; my dad's been saying it each time Casey comes up, like he has to say it out loud or he might forget it, too. I look at him now, hoping for support. He puts down his phone.

"I just think you're getting into this so quickly, when you usually..." Mom drops something in the sink. "I just don't want you rushing into anything," she says then. "I don't want him to distract you from..."

"From what?"

She turns around, shakes her head. "It's just so new," she says. "And he's not really your type, is he? Your usual type, I mean."

I open my mouth, but I don't have a response for this; it's not like I've had a Hunk of Nateness before, and I haven't told her much about Casey. Maybe because I knew this would happen. *Did* I know this would happen? It didn't happen with any of the guys I went out with before. I guess they weren't this *type*.

I swallow and try to slow my breathing. "What would he *distract* me from?" I repeat.

My dad stops her from answering this time. It's his quieter voice from across the table that reminds me my fists are clenched, my whole body tight.

"How do you feel about him?" Dad asks.

"I'm dating him." My voice is calmer now. Stronger. 'Dating' doesn't say everything, though. It feels right now like it says almost nothing.

"I don't want her to see him this weekend," Mom says, but to my dad, not to me. "She needs to stay home. To focus on her recovery."

They look at each other then like I'm not here. I think I see something else between them, something new. Something bad, something wrong.

And something *is* wrong, I know, something they won't tell me. Because I can't just will these seams in my body to close up with focus, can't mend bruised bones and grow new hair and let my brain get back to normal by sitting here thinking about it. You don't need a medical degree to know this.

I look at my dad, waiting for him to contradict her, but he doesn't, and I go to my room before they can say anything else.

Later, I text Casey, not about this, and just talking to him about odd things, things that don't matter, helps. I at least stop obsessing over what my parents aren't saying, and as I'm getting ready for bed, I remind myself I can play their game, too.

27

Casey

It feels like Saturday takes several days. It's like I'm living in the wrong reality, like some other-me is somewhere else doing what I'm supposed to be doing now. Where I should be, with Mischa. But this isn't a missing feeling, isn't a wanting feeling, isn't even a needing feeling. It's not lust or puppy love or whatever Nate and Bimi have that makes them want to be together every second, either. It's just that Mischa's there, and I'm here, and this is wrong.

"You're not resting," Ellen says when I come back downstairs late in the afternoon.

Resting. Right. That's what I said I was doing. Because I didn't sleep last night. It's not like I was having nightmares, though, like she thought. There wasn't any sleep for nightmares.

She turns away from the stove and looks at me. They're making veggie burgers tonight since Bimi's here for dinner and she liked them so much last time. Or Ellen is. Usually Rick makes them with her.

"I'm not tired," I repeat. I'm starting to sound like Mischa, how she's always having to convince everybody she's okay.

Ellen wrinkles her nose. I've already had a cup of her lavender tea that was supposed to help me relax. I'll probably drink half a gallon of it before I go to bed tonight and it still won't do anything. But not sleeping isn't really the problem; it's like after I didn't sleep those first nights at the hospital, my body adjusted and I don't need to anymore.

When Ellen doesn't say anything else, I go find Bimi and Nate. I knock on the door to the TV room before I open it, but there's no answer.

"They're out for a walk," Rick says, poking his head out of the den. "You want a coffee before dinner?"

"I just had a bunch of lavender tea."

He laughs. "Decaf, then," he says, "so Ellen doesn't get after you for that, too."

There's a smaller coffee maker in the den for Rick, one of the older ones that doesn't have the espresso stuff or the blue screen like Ellen's. Rick gets a new bag of grounds out from a cabinet and dumps it into the filter.

"It's not baseball," I tell him before I sit.

"I know," he says.

The pot sputters. "I'm not stressed," I add.

Rick studies me for a second. "You're supposed to be at Mischa's. That's what it is, isn't it?"

"That's exactly it," I say. And it really is this simple, a *supposed to be* and a *not*. I'm so sure of the *supposed to*. Not because I think something bad might happen this time. Not because I'm traumatized, either, or like I have implacable—I remember Ellen's word, because it was one Mischa might have used—fears or whatever because of what happened last week. Not even because I feel guilty about not getting there earlier, about not being able to stop it from happening.

"I understand," Rick says. "You said her parents are just...what'd Mischa say they were?"

I get out my phone. She texted it this morning. "Helicoptering," I read. She didn't understand why. It's not about her grades, about her getting behind or anything. And they can't be worried about how well she's healing. That's going so much better than the doctors expected.

Rick rolls his eyes. "Parents," he says, and we both try to laugh.

A couple hours later, Rick's doing the dishes while Ellen's sitting at the island massaging her temples—because obviously, *she's* the one who's tired. It's migraines, she told us, but she didn't eat much at dinner.

It's just me, Bimi, and Nate left at the table now, prom-planning.

"You should text Mischa about that," I tell Bimi when I haven't been paying attention to what they've been saying for a while. I think they're on pictures now. "Or we could call her."

"You know how she likes the arboretum." Bimi says this like her line about Jade's salty Chinese food and dress-bloating.

I get out my phone, and Bimi and Nate keep talking while I text Mischa.

Bimi thinks it's an inescapable fact of the universe that you can't eat noodles at Jade without busting out of your prom dress, I tell her.

She writes back right away with a laughing face. *Absolutely*, she says.

And that you want pictures at the arboretum.

That's good, she says, then, *I wish I were there with you all tonight.*

Me, too. I click the emoji button and scroll through all the faces and shapes. I stop on the hearts. My finger's hovering over the plain red one when Nate kicks my leg under the table. I look up.

"Carpooling," he says.

Ellen chimes in on that. "Give them the Lincoln," she tells Rick. "The girls need the leg room for their dresses."

Rick's putting soap in the dishwasher. "I don't know if it'll be done yet," he says as he stands up.

"Done?" Ellen asks.

"It's just a dent," he says. "It's from a driver when we had his car in for service."

"You let someone drive it?"

He shrugs. "Low stock on the leased cars." Then he looks over at us. "I can rush it, get it in on Monday so it'll be ready. The dent's small."

"Do that," Ellen tells him, "and make sure it's clean."

Bimi thanks them, and then she and Nate go back to their planning.

Everything must be okay, I keep telling myself, since I just keep going back to the hearts on my phone—plain hearts, hearts with arrows, hearts with sunbeams, vibrating hearts. But something still feels wrong.

I'm wide awake when Mischa goes to bed at nine. Bimi confirmed this. "In bed," she told me, holding up her phone while she was lying across Nate on the sofa like a very long cat.

I close the door behind them, then get my keys from the bowl in the hallway and shove my feet into some shoes by the front door. Because I don't think about these things anymore when they come to me. Not after finding her in the street.

"Going somewhere?" Rick asks. He's in the doorway of the den again.

"Just out," I tell him.

He nods like maybe he understands this and says he'll leave the light on for me.

I don't know how I know where to find her. At first, I think I'm imagining her on the bench at the park that looks over the pond. She must have walked all the way from the other lot.

But she's already turned around when I pull in, already looking this way when my low beams catch her.

"You knew it was me," I say as soon as I get out. I try not to slam the door. It's still too loud. The place is quiet otherwise.

Mischa nods.

"You're okay?" I ask. "Did something happen at..."

"Nothing," she says.

I sit down, and our hands go to each other. Because this is natural, right.

She's looking at me. "How'd you know?" she asks.

I want to tell her that I *didn't* know, but this would be a lie; I knew where I was going as soon as I got in the truck.

"You snuck out?" I ask.

She laughs. I feel my back release then, my shoulders relax.

"Something like that," she says.

I don't ask her why. She probably needed a break from whatever's going on with her parents. Maybe that's something that happens with parents when they're the biological kind, that too much of the same blood in a house can make it go sour.

"I didn't drive," she says. "I came through the woods. I would have texted you, but..."

"Your mom reads your texts."

Mischa sits back. "Maybe," she says. "I hadn't thought about it before, but she's been on her computer a lot, and she could see them on the family account. I just didn't want you to worry."

I squeeze her hand, but she feels real, solid. Maybe I

should be worried, but that's not what I was feeling when I left the house, not what I was feeling when I drove here. And there's nothing wrong when I'm with her. Runaway cars and beeping machines and youth pastors feel far away now.

We go quiet then. I don't know how long we sit looking out over the pond, a dark velvet mirror that ripples in the moonlight whenever the wind picks up. Some geese drift by, darker shadows against the shimmer.

Mischa keeps her hand in mine, and this feeling is enough, I think, that I could stay here with her forever and not miss anything outside of us. Her head falls against my shoulder after a while, and I set my arm behind her and try to pretend that time isn't passing.

Mischa doesn't move again until some clouds have turned the sky a milky blue. The wind's stronger now, whistling through the trees around the walking path.

"Thank you," she murmurs as she sits up.

"I didn't do anything."

"You did," she tells me. Her hair's blown around her cheek. "I feel better now."

I tell her I do, too, and I want to tell her it's all her, that I'll always feel better, will always feel *right* when I'm with her. But it's a lot to take in that everything's wrong when

I'm not, and I won't waste this time with her by thinking about what could be wrong later.

I think she's going to move and this is going to be over, but instead, she keeps my hand and lies back against my chest, turning so her spine's against me. Her eyes are closed, and I can count her breaths like this. This feels so different than when I was counting her breaths in the hospital. It's like there's nothing but the two of us on this bench now, nothing ahead of us or behind us that could mean anything.

Maybe she falls asleep. Maybe she's just still. It must be a while, because the moon's disappeared by the time she sits up. But it goes too quickly; it only feels like a few minutes have passed before we're both standing up again.

She tells me she doesn't want a ride home in case her parents are still awake but that she'll flash her bedroom lights when she gets in if I'll drive by. Not because she's scared of walking through the woods or because either of us are worried about what's out there, about *who's* still out there who might hurt her; I know she's safe. This is just another goodnight, and I know, as I walk her back to her side of park—taking our time, going slowly—that I want all of Mischa Kenning-Elliott's goodnights.

She stops close to the parking lot where a little patch of

concrete runs off into the dirt. As soon as I step down and the leaves rustle up around my ankles, it's like I'm rooted to the ground through the soles of my shoes, like it's trying to hold me here.

So I don't move. She doesn't, either, and it takes me a while—too long—to reach for her hand. I should have reached for her before; she's too far away now. I can't see her face and can barely make out half of her silhouette against the grass of the park. Her other half's a shadow that seems to stretch back forever into the woods.

"Can I kiss you?" I ask, but it's not my voice, not my body, I think, when she steps forward into me.

My lips find hers even though I can't see her, and it makes me feel like I'm half of something else then, not just me anymore.

I have to remember I don't have weak knees. I don't run out of breath running the bleachers at practice or overheat in the later innings when it's 95 and my hair's matted in sweat under my cap.

But this is different. When it stops, I can't catch my breath, and my heart's racing. I have one hand up against a tree, the other around Mischa. She laughs as she pulls a leaf from her hair, and then too soon after, she's gone.

I sprint back to my truck and get to the cul de sac off Magnolia a minute before she flashes her bedroom lights.

28

Mischa

After the park, I think my dreams are going to be sweet, but instead, they take me to the room again. I know it from the other dreams, but it feels like I'm remembering it from before them, too, like I've known it for so much longer. The shimmer in the walls feels blinding this time, and the floor's soft but looks almost like ice. There's no source of light that I can see, no bulbs in the ceiling or sconces or anything. It's like it's coming from everywhere.

And it should be beautiful, I think, that this should be a different kind of dream. But it feels like these shimmering walls are airtight. I remind myself to breathe. I can; there's nothing wrong with my body, at least, even asleep.

It's my head, these thoughts I can't stop even though I know I'm dreaming. I keep looking at the far wall. I have to go through it. It feels so important. But obviously, I can't walk through a wall.

I move closer to it this time, but I wake up before I reach it.

I'm not sweaty when I finally get out of bed at my usual time Sunday morning. I must look better, too.

"You look rested," Mom says when I come down for breakfast a little after nine. "Did you sleep better?"

I tell her I did. I want to tell her why, to tell her that I'm feeling *well*, even. It feels so strange to keep a secret from her, especially a secret that's good.

That afternoon, I have to stop myself from calling Casey. Mom's around all day, and she'd hear me even if she didn't see it on the account. Dad's out running errands, so it's just us in the house, and I can hear her footsteps everywhere she goes.

It's raining, so I decide to work on my thesis, and I'm through a draft and reading over to edit it when she taps on my door a little after four.

"I just wanted to check that you're all right," she says.

I save my changes and try to summon a voice that doesn't give anything away. "Just finishing my thesis," I tell her.

But this doesn't help; if anything, Mom looks even more worried. She doesn't leave.

"I'm good," I add, in case saying it again will help. But apparently I can't just be good anymore; I'm supposed to be something else, something worse. I don't know why my parents are so attached to this, to something being wrong, to me being sick. More sick than I was before, I mean, with lupus, and when I feel like I'm so much better.

"Can I come in?" she asks.

I pull back my chair and leave the text document up on my laptop. There's nothing to hide in my thesis, at least.

"I've been thinking a lot about your situation," Mom says when I think she's just going to stand there.

I steel myself for this. "My situation?" I ask, managing to keep the teenager out of my voice. But maybe I should be doing the opposite, rolling my eyes and putting all the teenager I have into this. Maybe that would make this talk better. Maybe that would make this talk *normal*, at least.

"Don't be like that," Mom says, obviously assuming the teenager tone anyway. She sits on the corner of my bed how she used to when something was wrong, back when I wanted her here. When she made things seem better instead of worse.

"I'm on your side, Mischa," she says. "I want things to go smoothly for you. I want what's best for you."

"Casey," I say, because it has to be Casey she thinks

isn't what's best for me. It can't be that I'm doing too much homework or that I'm not resting enough or not eating well. She wasn't this way before Casey. "You don't want me to see Casey."

She says it's not that, of course, not him specifically, and stumbles around all the usual well-intentioned maternal worries, the concerns she thinks she's supposed to have about me at seventeen that have never really applied in my case. She repeats herself a few times about not being *against* Casey, exactly. She's more *pro-me*, she says, the way adults do when they want to pretend they don't have an opinion about something so you can come around to their idea and think it was yours.

But this doesn't work on me anymore. I'm not sure it ever really worked on me; we just used to agree more often. In the middle of a talk about the changes in my life, the way junior years are always stressful, she winds her way back to, "Since you bring him up..."

I try to keep my face still, my voice easy. "Casey?" I ask, like I might have forgotten why we're here.

Mom looks over her shoulder at my open door, then at me again. "How well do you know him?" she asks. "You...you really haven't told me anything about him."

"Well." It comes out before I can stop it. "I know him well. For how long I've known him, I mean."

"You...you've..." She stops. "You're...serious?"

Oh my god, my brain screams, full screeching teenager in a cheesy horror who's about to be stabbed with a meat cleaver in a basement. *Is this a sex talk? Please let this not be a sex talk*, I think, then, considering this, *please let this only be a sex talk*. Because that's at least something I can navigate, something I know what to do with. And isn't that what should happen now?

But this isn't going to be a sex talk, I know. My mom wasn't anxious like this when she ordered an anatomical woman for us to put together when I was ten and she talked to me about menstruation for the first time. 'Menstruation' was the word she used, post 'ovulation,' with 'uterine shedding.' It took me three more years to figure out what that kind of period was. My mom doesn't shy away from sex talk.

So this is something worse, something bigger. I try to head her off, to say that we're really *not* serious, Casey and I. Because for the purposes of this conversation, it doesn't matter that this isn't true.

"Okay," Mom says. She picks at a fingernail. "Okay. I was just wondering if...you know, it seemed like it was kind of sudden."

"Sudden?" I ask, because I'm seventeen, and I've dated before. It always feels sudden and kind of weird at the beginning. Except this, with Casey. This doesn't feel sudden at all. When I'm with him, it feels like we're something old, something sure. But I can't say this.

Mom's looking at me now like I'm someone different. Like Kafka's character, I think, who turned into a giant bug. But wasn't that about alcoholism? I don't drink. Casey doesn't drink, either. I try telling her *this*, at least, to make some promise I can keep and show her I'm not suddenly going to lose myself, to become someone different than I've been all along.

She shakes her head, but she's looking at my door now, not at me. "I know," she says. "I know that about you. But about him..."

I'm trying to be honest then when I tell her that this relationship feels good, feels safe. And it seems like she should feel good about it, too, since it was Casey who picked me up from the road, Casey who drove me to the hospital and saved my life. But my mom's getting more shifty the longer I talk about him. There's something wrong, suddenly, with things going well, with dating just being easy for me for the first time.

"*Too* easy," she cuts in. "Don't you feel like..." She doesn't finish. She doesn't have to. Maybe she's thinking what I am, what I was about to tell Casey when I was hit by the car—that *I* might be what's wrong in this, that it might be something in me, something that's happening to me, that's *gotten* to me, like Pastor Dave said, and this relationship is wrong. Because of the occult Kaitlen keeps talking about or whatever. I want to think it really is just a *whatever* and let it roll off me like *whatever*s should at this age.

I take inventory of my body then, the way she—Mom, before all this—taught me. But nothing feels wrong. Everything with Casey's felt right from the start. The dreams of him are the ones I want to have, the ones I don't want to give up. I guess that's it, that I don't want this to be wrong so badly that it feels like my whole world is riding on this one thing being right.

I don't know if my mom can see this on my face. She finally says something about mothers just worrying and leaves me alone.

In case she's reading my texts, I wait to write Casey back for a little while when he asks how I'm doing. It's almost funny, I think, that it's my mom I'm playing these games with now instead of my boyfriend.

Bimi texts just before dinner with a *We missed you last night.*

Me, too, I say. *Next weekend.* I add a heart. Then I decide to test this. *Want to get our nails done Tuesday after school?* I ask.

She sends a thumbs up.

*   *

Monday morning, I get up early and take my time eating my oatmeal at the kitchen island while Mom watches me. It's rainy today, drops pelting the windows in a steady patter.

"You're sure you're up for a full day of school?" she asks. "You know they said they could give you more days."

"Absolutely."

"You're not still feeling tired from the..."

"Nope."

She sighs one of her exasperated Mom sighs. I think she got it from those dish detergent commercials about water spots and she hasn't considered yet that raising a teenager woes should sound different than the stereotypically middle-aged plague of spotty glassware.

"I'm actually excited," I tell her. "You know, because it's prom week." Because that's what seventeen-year-olds are supposed to be excited about, isn't it, junior prom? But I guess Mom's never said she wanted me to be *normal,* exactly.

I wait to mention getting my nails done until she has her keys in her hand, since she's driving me again. Though I don't think the doctors said anything about not letting me drive. She's a few steps ahead of me, so maybe I time this wrong, not being able to see her face.

"Bimi'll bring me home after school," I say as I'm putting on my shoes. "We're going to get manicures."

Mom taps at the garage door button that always sticks. She's by the car before she responds. "I thought you said that was Tuesday," she says.

"Did I?" I ask, and make a show of checking my texts when I get in. "Right," I tell her. "You're right. Tuesday."

So she's definitely reading my texts. She must have checked the account even since last night. I try to control the anger that causes a flash of heat all through me, to keep my face still and my voice bored as she asks some things about my classes.

When we finally pull up to the front steps, I tell her Casey will give me a ride home after baseball and slam my door closed before she can respond.

29

Casey

Monday morning, I get to the weight room about half an hour before the others. The locker room window's still dark when I'm getting out of the shower around the time they unlock the doors upstairs.

Perkins comes in as I'm getting dressed. "Shit," he says when he sees me. Because I'm never *this* early. "What's wrong?"

I shrug and tell him I was just awake. Some of the other guys are changing out now. "You all good?" I ask.

He nods. The team's been pumped up and jittery; they're feeling this Friday's away games already, a double with Greenville and Salem. After last week, we should win both. And Sturgis has gotten a last-minute prom date, he tells everybody, Angela Milton.

When Miller and some of the others move out into the hall, I can hear them kicking around one of those weird pink and orange puff things that look like fuzzy kickballs—some kind of sea creature, I think, because this year's prom's an underwater theme. Apparently that's why Kaitlen and her student council minions dumped a bunch of sparkly blue curtains in front of the stairs, too. You have to get a running start to jump over all of them, and there's glitter trailing all down the pool hall.

"Mischa okay?" Perkins asks once our bay of lockers has cleared out.

"All right," I tell him. Because that's what she keeps telling me. She's had kind of miracle recovery, one of her doctors said, from all that good luck they think stayed with her. It pisses me off, everybody saying this was luck. You're not lucky just because the person trying to kill you hasn't finished the job yet.

My hand's still on my locker when I realize Perkins is looking at me. "You're worried about her," he says. "You want us to walk with you? You're gonna carry her books between classes, aren't you?"

"Right," I say. "Because of the stitches in her shoulder. She can't bring a bag. But I've got it, thanks."

He nods, but he doesn't leave until I'm walking out the doors, too.

I kick one of the fuzzy pink things back into the storage room. "You're ready to pitch, aren't you?" I ask. "In case I can't Friday?"

Perkins whips around to face me. "Your arm," he says.

"It's fine."

"You should rest it. Don't take any chances."

"You, either," I tell him as I take the stairs two at a time. "Be ready to pitch."

Mischa's smiling one of those fake smiles for everybody in the hallways today. I keep looking over my shoulder for Dave or for anybody else who could hurt her, but of course there aren't any cars in the Centerville hallways, and everybody seems to know to give her space.

My teachers are all letting me out of classes early so I can get to her rooms to grab her books from her desk and take them to her next class. She's got a ton, and she's not supposed to carry more than one at a time. It's just a precaution, she says, for her back and her stitches, but none of it felt like a precaution when they had her on that board going into surgery. It was like she was falling apart, like it was just the board and a bunch of straps holding her together. And they didn't think then that they'd be able to keep her together.

I try to stop thinking about this, to look at her the way

she is now, with her ponytail hiding the shaved spot at the back of her head and her stitches starting to dissolve on her cheek.

She tells me she's all right over and over, just like she tells her teachers—that she's feeling fine, like herself, that she's up to being back at school full time.

It's not until lunch, when the others are talking about prom, that her smile breaks and she says she needs to talk to me. After school, she says, if I don't have to go to practice right away.

I tell her this is no problem and do my best not to look scared shitless.

I leave Government early to tell Greene I'll be late for practice. But I must not look right; he tells me to just skip today if I'm not feeling up to it. My arm and all that. I should ice it again, he says, and just do some slow throwing with Aarons if I do anything.

It isn't like Greene, and I wonder if he wants me to rest my head more than my arm, if he knows my head's what might snap now.

Mischa looks tired by the time I meet her after her Precalc class. I look behind us a few times as we head for her favorite log in the woods, but there's no one around.

It's a little cooler once we get down under the trees, and she says something about the mud and my new shoes.

"They're fine," I tell her.

"You're sure you won't be late for practice?" she asks.

"What's wrong?"

She's craning her neck to see over the hill, towards the fields. "The guys are excited about Friday, huh?" She keeps walking down into the creek with the tree across it, where nobody could see us even from the back of the field.

"I don't have to go," I tell her.

"What?"

"To the games, if..."

"No," she says.

I wait for her to sit down. "The team'll be home Friday night. Is there something you wanted to..."

"It's not that," she says and gestures for me to sit next to her.

I set my backpack on the ground and balance her Precalc book on top. My hands are shaking; it takes me a couple tries. "Is it prom?" I ask as I sit down, squeezing my hands together to stop them from moving. "We can stay home if you want. We don't have to go."

She's meeting my eyes now, at least, but there's something wrong on her face. Obviously wrong, I mean, big wrong. She's not trying to hide it anymore. So I wait. I want to yell, want to scream at someone, instead. Not at her. But that's what this silence feels like, like screaming in my head.

"My mom's reading my texts," she says, finally.

I let out a breath. *Is that all?* I want to ask. But that's not what I mean, that this shouldn't matter to her. "I'm sorry," I say when I think she wants me to say something.

She takes my hand. I didn't realize I'd balled it into a fist. "I don't know why she's doing this all of a sudden," she says. "But she's been asking about...about you, actually."

I wait for her to say more, but it doesn't matter if it's me or if it's something else her mom's after or if I should have seen this coming. If I *did* see this coming, even, back in the hospital, how Lisa didn't trust me. What matters is that she went from being an assumed *for* Mischa to an *against* Mischa. I'm struck by how black and white this is, how simple. For or against. Friend or foe. It's like teams, like this is a game. I don't need any more information.

It's not that way for Mischa, though, and it pisses me off that there's someone who could do this to her. So I let her talk through it, trying not to push her in any direction. But she already has a plan.

"I want to keep it from her," she says.

"It?"

"Us." She looks away, back towards the fields. Her face is flushed. "I mean..."

"Okay," I say.

She looks at me. "It's okay with you?" she asks. "Really?"

I tell her of course it is, that it's whatever's easiest for her. Whatever lets *us* keep going, I guess I mean, too.

We're quiet for a minute, her leaning back to watch some birds hopping between the tree branches.

"I'm going to tell her we're fizzling out," she says.

"Okay."

"A lie," she adds, looking down at my hand in hers. "I'll have Bimi say I'm going over to her house Friday instead of to yours and Nate's when you get back from the games. We'll text that so my mom gets it, too."

"Bimi's on board with this?" I ask, when I really want to ask if she's sure she can trust Bimi.

Mischa nods. "She will be. I just wanted to run it by you first."

I wait for her to say something else, but it's just the birds chirping then, rustling around in the leaves starting to bud out on the branches.

"You're comfortable with that?" I ask her. "Lying to your mom?"

"I am," she says, and twists to lay her head against my

shoulder. "I think it's best, at least until after prom."

I rest my chin on her forehead. "Good," I say, and I let this be enough, like her dad said that first night in the hospital, that we'll deal with after, after.

30

Mischa

Like we planned, I don't text Casey Monday night, and by the time I'm getting ready for school Tuesday morning, I wish I'd emailed him, instead. Just because I want to vent about how weird my mom's being. But maybe she reads my emails, too. I leave my gmail account up on the laptop all the time, so maybe there's nothing that's safe from her.

I try to keep everything—my face, my voice, even my body—neutral as I have my oatmeal and she asks her usual questions. I tell her about my paper again, about madness in Poe's and Gilman's narrators like there isn't a kind of madness in me now, too.

"You look like you slept better," is all she says.

It's the concealer working, I think, just layering on more of it. But of course she knows I didn't text Casey last night, so this is probably what she wants to see, what she's looking for.

"Yeah," I tell her.

She nods. "That's good." I almost think she's really going to lie now and say I look happier, too, *better* somehow, like the me she thinks I'm supposed to be, sans Casey. She waits until we're in the car to ask about him, though, how "everything's going" in that department.

"Fine," I tell her, then, after a pause, "I guess."

She takes the turn too quickly onto Magnolia and almost runs over Mrs. Phillips' roses that are starting to bloom again. "You guess?" she prompts once we've straightened out.

I keep my eyes on the road. "I don't know. It's...fine."

"That doesn't sound good," Mom says quickly.

I fiddle with my purse strap. "It's not a big deal. We're maybe just kind of fizzling out."

She exhales. "A natural end," she says, then a fake, "I'm sorry to hear that."

"Sure," I say.

There are too many people around to overhear us when I get to the pool hallway, so I have to wait to talk to Bimi about the plan for this weekend until we're in line for lunch. The cafeteria's loud, and I can barely hear my thoughts. Prom week's always weird like this, though, sort of extra buzzy.

Bimi's gone into two collective *we's* now, the *we* that includes me and Casey and the *we* that's just her and Nate. At least she's not calling him Hunk of Nateness anymore. Because they're serious now, she says. I tell her I understand, even though theirs seems like such a different kind of 'serious' than what Casey and I are.

Once we're waiting off to the side of the line for the next pizza box and she's talking about her high tech strapless bra, it takes me a couple tries to get out that I can't go to prom with her and Nate Saturday night.

I swear Bimi's eyes bug out of their sockets. Like the Kafka book, I guess, like Gregor. Like a bug.

"*With* you, with you guys, I mean," I say quickly.

Bimi starts vibrating, her ponytail shimmying behind her shoulders. "*What?*" she sputters after a few seconds, and I half expect her to explode with the verbal equivalent of diarrhea. But she just keeps vibrating.

I hurry through this. "I can still meet you at the dance, but I have to *say* I'm not going with you. With Casey, I mean."

"*What?*" she repeats, an octave higher this time.

"It's okay," I tell her, pulling her a little farther from the line and almost into the kitchens. "It's just what I have to tell my mom. And I need you to help me keep it from her that I'm still seeing Casey at all."

It takes Bimi a second to swallow. She opens her mouth in a *w* and I think is about to say 'what' again when she shakes her head. "Your mom?" she asks.

But she goes back to vibrating as I explain the Mom-reading-my-texts-and-being-anti-Casey situation.

There's a pause when I finish. "Shit," she says then.

I try to tell her this is okay. That I'm okay, at least, that *we're* okay. But maybe I'm wrong. *Is* this shit? I've never had to lie to my mom before.

"Why?" Bimi demands when our pizza box finally comes out. "Why would she *not* be into him? He's *Casey Everfeld.*"

I think about this as we walk the rest of the way through the line.

"*Why*?" Bimi asks again, quieter this time, when we're getting our napkins.

I tell her I don't know, and she looks at me over her shoulder like maybe I'm lying to her now, too.

"So about Friday night at their place..." I say, because we'd already planned another movie night, another *chilling*, as she calls it.

Bimi stops and spins to face me. I almost run into her with my tray. "Don't tell me you're not coming," she says, then, before I can answer, "That's *shit.*"

"No. I am."

She hmphs before continuing on towards our table. I look at the hallway just as Casey's coming in. He smiles at me. I can't help but smile back, and this should feel wrong, I think, with what I've just been talking about. But it doesn't.

"So I'll text you about coming over to your place, instead," I tell Bimi as we're sitting down. Maybe I shouldn't still be smiling.

"Got it," Bimi says. "But it's still shit."

That night, my new French tips shining under the pendant lights in the kitchen, we eat cheesy lasagna and homemade peach ice cream—my favorite, a guilt dessert. My mom and dad watch me from across the table as I'm spooning the last of the soupy ice cream from my bowl.

"School going all right?" Dad asks, finally thinking of something non-Casey related to say to me.

I try to remember I'm supposed to be depressed about Casey, not pissed at my parents. But maybe these look about the same, teenager-style. "Okay," I say, perfectly neutral.

He looks at my mom.

"We're here if you want to talk about it," she says.

I decide on a shrug this time. I wonder if I look

indifferent enough, if I'm pulling this off.

"I've thought about prom," I tell them, and wait, watching my mom out of the corner of my eye as I push my ice cream bowl away.

"*And*?" she prompts.

"I'm going alone. I'll meet up with Bimi there."

"That's good," Dad says at the same time Mom says, "Won't she be with Nate?"

I try to keep my face still. I'm not sure if it's wanting to smile or smirk, or something worse. Probably something worse. "Nate and Casey aren't that close," I tell her. "Casey'll be with the baseball guys, so it won't be awkward."

"You know, it's good to go alone," Dad says, sounding almost like I imagine a parent should about prom. "Down the road, I mean, with pictures, you'll be glad you didn't have some date whose name you can't remember." He says this like I could ever *not* remember Casey Everfeld's name.

"And you don't *have to* go at all," Mom says. She rolls her eyes. "*Junior prom.*"

I stare at my empty ice cream bowl as she tells us about hers, about how much better senior prom is all around. Dad adds his own story about a date he spilled punch on who wouldn't speak to him the rest of the night. I'm not missing anything, they assure me, if I skip my junior prom altogether. It's how they used to talk to me about the sports I couldn't play in the heat because of the lupus and about the candy I couldn't eat. Nothing I was missing out on.

So I guess I've trained for this, in a way. I think I keep control of my face well enough while I rinse off my dishes, and then I tell them I'm tired. And of course they support my going up to bed early, because tired is all they ever think I should be.

31

Casey

Wednesday morning, Rick's already in the kitchen and has Ellen's coffee maker going when I come downstairs.

"Early workout?" he asks.

I nod and get my cereal from the pantry. "You're up early," I say.

He's sitting at the table watching me. He wants to talk, and I know this won't be a good talk; it takes something important to get Rick out of bed before the sun's up.

"What is it?" I ask.

For a second, I think he's going to lie. "News from the station," he says, finally. "Officer Melton. He's the one who always stops by for donuts on his way into town."

I curse under my breath when I slam my finger in the drawer with the spoons.

"They still haven't got anything on the car that hit Mischa," Rick says.

"I knew that," I tell him. So this can't be what he wants to talk about.

He shrugs. "'s all I know."

But it's not all he knows. I can see it. I set my bowl on the table and keep looking at him as I sit down.

"It's just I don't think they've got any leads," he says.

I'm glad I'm not holding anything in my hands now. They fist in my lap. "That's shit." I'm starting to sound like Bimi.

Rick doesn't correct me. "I'm sorry. But there hasn't been anything at school since she's been back? She hasn't seen Dave or..."

"No."

Rick opens his mouth like he's going to say something else, like he's going to tell me this is a good sign or maybe try to comfort me or something. But he doesn't. He just dumps some coffee in a to-go mug for me when it's time and says he's here if I ever need to vent.

When her mom drops her off, I meet Mischa away from the windows of the atrium like she asked so her mom doesn't see. Mischa says she's fine, that she told her parents about going to prom alone and everything went all right. But *too* all right, I think, that it can't be this easy.

I take the book she's holding and open my arms like I'm going to hug her—do I hug her, now, in the mornings? I don't know. I feel like I can finally take a full breath, though, when she leans into me, wraps her arms around my back and squeezes for just a second before she pulls away and looks at my face.

"You're okay?" I ask. "With..."

"With everything," she finishes for me.

Through the day, Mischa at least acts okay. She smiles a lot and never jumps when there's yelling in the hallways or when somebody drops something. Like Chad Frederickson, who dropped his lunch tray right behind her. Mischa just kept on eating her cookie. It bothered me, not her. Or maybe it bothered me that it *didn't* bother her, that she's not ready if somebody really does pop out from around some corner, somebody who wants to hurt her.

I like seeing her happy, though, like seeing her talking to Bimi about prom and slaying her thesis and forgetting about where she's missing hair at the back of her head like she hasn't just been through hell, like she really is okay.

So it doesn't seem weird to me when I'm the one

watching from behind a corner when she gets into her mom's car after school. After they pull out of the lot, I go straight for Greene.

He's in his office, an empty mug of coffee on his desk and papers with batting lists scattered all over. He flinches when I knock, then tells me to sit. He always starts to get jumpy around this time of year, but I think it might be worse now that we actually have a shot at state. It's the pressure, he says. Like what he thinks I'm under. What everybody thinks I'm under, even though they're all wrong.

"You need to play Perkins," I tell him before he can say anything to me.

He drops his pen. It bounces off his desk, and he doesn't pick it up. I think he'll probably yell, looking at his face, but then he just shakes his head and leans back in his chair.

"This is no time to be generous," he says. "You know that scout..."

"No," I say. Because I'm not being generous. I haven't got the jitters, either, and I don't give a shit about the scout coming to Greenville on Friday. "Play Perkins. If something goes wrong, play Miller, even, if you have to."

Greene shakes his head. "You've got too much pressure," he says. "Are you startin' to get..."

"I'm fine. It's not my arm." But I don't know what to

tell him it is. I can't tell him the truth, that I'm not going to be at state. It's not that I'm stressed, though, or that my arm's getting sticky; I only care how it might affect the rest of the team if I'm not there. *When* I'm not there. I'm sure of it. I just can't tell him that. I can't even make sense of why I think it.

"Your workouts," Greene says. "Maybe we should hold back, have one of the PT's work with your arm."

"Workouts are fine. It's...it's just a backup plan."

Greene raises his eyebrows. Greene always has a backup plan. He taught me that. You need them in baseball.

"I just don't want to throw state for us if I get a jammed elbow or something in the middle of a game," I tell him.

He picks up the pen and starts chewing on the cap. "It's not a bad idea," he says after a second. "For now, anyway, to make sure you're not pushing it at these early games. We could split some innings with Perkins."

"Good," I say. "He's ready," but then I can feel Greene's eyes on my back as I go out and join the others in the locker room.

32

Mischa

We keep following the plan as the week goes on. At school, Casey's with me during every passing period, and I tell him the same things I tell my mom—that I'm feeling fine, that I'm sleeping well, that nothing's bothering me.

At home, I spend the evenings pretending to be thinking about anything but Casey and the nights in weird dreams. *Juggling* is what Bimi calls it. I'm just learning how to juggle truths.

Bimi, true to form, has already aced this. She's texted me about coming over to her place tomorrow twice since Tuesday, just in case my mom missed the first one or had any hint I might be going to the Everfelds' instead, like she's ever had any reason not to trust me. Like I've never had a reason not to trust her, I guess, before now. Maybe that's what's making everything feel off balance, the newness of it. I should have practiced lying to my parents before now; I only have a couple more years of teenage-hood left.

But things are easy at school, at least. The days fly by in a blur of classes that are all going smoothly, walks with Casey, and the prom energy that feels as physically present this week as the glitter that's spread from the pool hallway all down the Science department.

Thursday, our lunch table's split between talk about the games tomorrow at Greenville and Salem the baseball team's missing school for and dinner plans Saturday before the dance. The others in our group are all going to Mitch's house for pictures.

"What about you two?" Kirsten asks, turning to me and Casey when I'm lost somewhere between the two conversations.

"What?" I ask.

"Dinner Saturday. Before prom."

I look at Casey. But this is school, where we're together. Where we can still be together.

"We're staying in," he says smoothly.

"Kay," Kirsten says. "So you won't be over for pictures?"

Pictures. We won't have pictures together. I don't know why I didn't think of this before. We can't have pictures.

At least not the kind with our friends that would end up on Social or the ones the photographer will take of couples as they come in. They post them on the website my mom will be all over. But I don't know how to tell my friends this.

Casey answers, instead, saying something about doing our own thing just for this year.

"You won't be able to have prom pictures," I say when he's looking at me and everyone else is talking again.

He leans in. "Is that okay?" he asks.

I shake my head. And this is when it hits me. Not like I thought it would at the hospital or when I found out about my mom reading my texts. Not any of the times I might have seen it coming.

I get up and make a beeline for the bathroom, pushing my tongue to the roof of my mouth hard, like I can hold up the tears with just this force.

Casey's behind me then. He takes my elbow and leads me around an alcove by the pool staircase, and suddenly, all the noise of the cafeteria's gone when we turn again into a little brick storage hallway at the back. He has his arms around me by the time the tears come.

He doesn't say anything, and it takes a while for this to run its course. His hands are warm against my back when I finally lift my face off his shirt and catch my breath, telling him I'm sorry.

"Don't be," he says.

I lean back into him. "I don't know what that was."

"It doesn't matter," he says, "unless you want to talk about it."

But I don't. And I guess I am feeling better after, like those health class videos say you're supposed to after a good cry. Chemicals, Mr. Rose would say. They have to get out of the body somehow. It's like this was just a crying out of all the drugs from the hospital that had finally made their way to my tear ducts. And I tell myself it could have been something like this; it doesn't have to be the secrets I'm keeping, the fears I can't seem to shake. About Casey. About my dreams. About whatever's causing them, whatever's giving me this thing with him that I want so badly not to lose. And everything I already know that's changing because of it.

"I can stay home," he says. "I really don't have to go with the team tomorrow. I'll tell Greene I'm sick, or that I need to rest my arm, and..."

"No," I say, because I can't take baseball from him, too.

For a second, I think he might argue. But I can't take any argument now. I can't even take prom talk, apparently, the happy kind, without crying. I never thought of myself as delicate before this, even when everyone else did. I guess that's changed, too.

"If you're sure," he says, finally.

I keep my face at his chest, breathing him in, and a minute later, I feel better. I tell him I'm okay to go back as I run my fingers under my eyes to check for stray eyeliner. But it's like the bags aren't even there anymore, like I really am healing quickly, even from tears.

Casey says I look fine, good. Like this never happened. He keeps my hand as we walk back to our table.

Bimi catches my eye before I get to my chair, and Nate pushes my cookies towards me. He's still getting them for me every day so I don't have to face Kaitlen. Bimi looks at Casey when we sit down like he might give something more away about what this was, but he doesn't. He just keeps my hand and waits for me to join back in the conversation.

I'm turning to the clock to check the time—the bell should ring soon—when Casey snatches the cookie out of my hand.

"What..." I can't get any more out. There's screaming from behind me, and it takes me a second to stand and see it. Someone's on the ground.

I look at Casey, down at my wrist he still has. The cookie's on the floor now.

"Nuts," he says.

That's what someone yells over by the cookie table, too. When one of the other teachers starts moving people back, I get a look at Sam Rodriguez's face just before Mrs. Hoffman stabs him with epinephrine.

"Nuts," Casey repeats. His voice is quiet, different—scary, I think I'd say some other time. "He's allergic to them. The way you are."

33

Casey

The blood's pounding at the sides of my head, and it's like I can focus on everything at once, on every word that seems to stretch out for too long, on every scrape of a chair from somebody getting up, on every freaking thing that moves anywhere near Mischa.

I try to just focus on her once there's enough space around her body that I know no one's coming towards her. I watch how she's breathing, how her spine's stiffened, how she's looking down now, at the cookie that fell on the floor. The cookie I knocked out of her hand.

"Nuts," I tell her when she looks at me again. I nod at Rodriguez, who's gone still on the floor. The school nurse is running over now. Somebody's called an ambulance. "He's allergic to them. The way you are." Not the give you hives or a stomachache way. The throat-closing, kill-you-fast-if-you-don't-have-your-epipen way.

Mischa doesn't respond, and I realize I still have her wrist. I'm squeezing it. I let go and tell her I'm sorry.

But she's looking at Rodriguez. So is everybody else. I swear I see every face in the room. It's Kaitlen Miller's I land on, though. Because Kaitlen Miller is the only person in this cafeteria who's looking at Mischa.

Rodriguez is all anybody in the halls can talk about as we're walking to Thesis. There's speculation about what happened to him, most of it far off the mark. Was there a wasp in that corner by the trash cans again? Did he miss some medication? Did he get a candy bar from the vending machine? I don't know why they couldn't hear it. 'Nuts' was all I could hear, all I could think.

I keep looking at Mischa, but this isn't for talking about right now. Not here, at least. I look for some sign she's watching the others the way I am, that she's waiting for someone to come after her with something bigger, something that's not hidden in a cookie. But she's steady, quiet like always, with that easy-looking smile plastered across her face that I know *isn't* easy, even back before anybody tried to kill her.

I try to make my face the same for now. But even if I could pull off Mischa's smile, my body gives me away; I'm shaking, vibrating inside. So I make sure not to touch her as we walk, to keep both my hands on our books even though they're not that heavy and not to let her see the way my whole body tenses up anytime somebody gets too close to her other side.

She asks if I'm okay when we get to Stevens' room.

"Fine," I tell her. I should have said something on the walk over. I look back at the doorway. Bimi and Nate were probably talking to us before they went the other way.

Kaitlen isn't here yet. Her chair's empty. I wait for Mischa to sit down, but she's still looking at me. I guess because I haven't had all her practice at putting on a face for other people.

She reaches for her Precalc book and then pulls some printed pages for her thesis out from behind the cover, saying she's just going to give them to Mrs. Stevens.

I watch her weave through the desks before Kaitlen comes in.

Of course Kaitlen smiles at me, and it takes everything in me to stay where I am. I suck in a breath and try to keep my voice even. Not screaming, at least. It's good this doesn't take many words. "The bench," I tell her. "Before practice. Meet me."

It's the way she keeps smiling. I have to walk away. So I circle over to Mrs. Stevens' desk and listen to her praise of Mischa's intro paragraph and her concern about how much work she's doing—all the things you'd expect, because it's Mischa.

When Mischa turns back to me, I try to pull off a smile, telling myself I can fix this feeling we're both having after seeing Rodriguez on the floor gasping for air, that I can make sure she's safe. And I will.

After last period, we go in the opposite direction as the crowd, and I swear I see Dave, Kaitlen, or some other threat in every face that passes us. The English hallway's cleared out by the time Mischa opens her locker.

I set her Precalc book inside and close the door, and she smiles that smile at me again and tells me she's all right. As we walk towards the atrium—too fast—she talks about tomorrow night with Bimi and Nate and how everything will be good then, how her mom hasn't figured out about her coming over after the games. Like lunch today never happened.

I try to keep this up, too, pretending. So she doesn't see anything wrong on my face, so she doesn't worry. Because Nate will carry her books while I'm at the games tomorrow. I already got a note for him. And then I'll be back and we'll have the evening together at home and prom the next night, even if we can't drive there together, and

Mischa will be safe. That's what matters, that Mischa's safe.

We stop at the brick wall with the stained glass bulldog and hug like this time we'll be apart is much longer. I watch her get in her dad's SUV through the bulldog's paw.

I wait until the car's around the corner on Main Street before I head for Kaitlen. I don't bother to go to the locker room first to change out. I can't risk any of the other guys coming with me.

Perkins is at the top of the stairs, and he tries to follow me when I blow by him. I tell him I'll be there in a few. This won't take long. And maybe he can see he shouldn't ask where I'm going.

Once I get through all the prom decorations and out the gym door, I run towards the field. It's like my skin's been on fire since the cafeteria, hot in that almost itching way that makes me want to crawl out of it. The heat's all through me when I get to Kaitlen standing by the bench. Fucking smiling.

I have to look away from her. I want to punch her. That's what I think first, my hands balled into fists before I know what they're doing, before I knew I could hit even somebody like Kaitlen Miller.

It's this that sinks in, that makes me take a breath, and then another, how you're supposed to breathe through anger. They called it rage in those groups for foster kids. Except I didn't know what rage was then.

I think Kaitlen must be able to see it when I stop short of her. "You did it," I say. I don't get out 'nuts' or 'cookies' or any of the other shit she doesn't need to hear to know exactly what I'm talking about.

She opens her mouth, but it's her eyes, the way they look at me, at the ground, back at me. She's going to lie.

I try to breathe, to wait. It takes a lot not to do something else now.

She does manage to say something after a while, but I don't hear it. All I can hear is the blood in my head now. I swear I can feel it pumping through my legs, my arms, even my fists that won't stop curling like I really am going to hit her.

I step back, because I know that I *could* hit her, when I tell her this will not happen again.

She's shrunk away. Because she sees this, obviously. And then I really do have to leave, have to sprint all the way back to the locker room and tell myself over and over that I'm not somebody who would hurt Kaitlen Miller. Except I am.

I throw too hard at practice, and Greene has me sit out the last half hour icing my arm on the bench and going over signs with Aarons. Because Greene doesn't know what this is, that I need more than some hard throws—even my fastest, even today—to get it out of me.

Afterwards, the guys are loud in the showers, and Rodriguez's name keeps coming up. Greene told us he was okay—stable, at least, still under observation at the hospital. I crank the water knob too hard, squeaking it, before I grab my towel and storm out when I can't stand hearing this anymore.

"You okay?" Perkins asks when he catches up to me at the lockers a minute later.

I focus on getting my jeans buttoned. There's still soap in my toes.

"You're ready for tomorrow," I tell him.

"Don't let it get to your head," he says. He's talking about Rodriguez, though, and Salem's winning streak this season, not about Kaitlen.

I blow by him and go to Greene.

"It was Kaitlen Miller," I say as soon as I open the door of his office. "She put the nuts in the cookies Rodriguez ate."

Greene doesn't catch up with me as I run down the hall and out into the heat again, because tonight, I don't have time for him, either.

34

Errands. Lisa told Stan she was running errands when she had him pick up Mischa from school. Because he wouldn't understand. He's never understood how important this is, how much could be at stake. Stan's never been as dedicated as she has to preparing their little girl for what she was meant to be.

Now it won't matter what he thinks about Mischa needing help from anyone, about the Everfeld kid being on their side—because he's wrong, Lisa's sure. Casey Everfeld is a threat. Or at least she thinks he is. If not, he's a distraction. Either way, he has to go; they can't afford any distractions.

All it took was Lisa waiting there in the trees her daughter thinks are hers. She had her phone out already when the bell rang, when she thought she probably wouldn't get this lucky and would only see Casey at practice. She never thought she'd catch him with a girl, and Kaitlen Miller to boot. Lisa takes this as confirmation, of course, that she's doing the right thing.

The pictures couldn't have turned out better. They're just the right angle to make it look like Casey's standing over Kaitlen. One's a little out of focus and makes Kaitlen look like she's pressed against his chest.

And that's enough, Lisa tells herself as she drives home. It has to be.

35

Mischa

The Sam Rodriguez cookie fiasco is all my parents want to talk about at dinner over our chicken breasts. If I saw anything. If I told anyone I was allergic to nuts other than the nurse's office and those forms you have to fill out with your doctor at the beginning of high school. If there's any chance the dough got contaminated somehow, the chocolate chip cookies that are supposed to be nut-free, just like everything else at Centerville is and those cookies have been every other day I've been there.

My mom keeps asking about the dough even after my dad lets off. *If it was meant for me* is what she means. And I don't know how to answer this.

Dad's on her side this time, chiming in with support when she decides I need to bring my lunch from now on. Starting tomorrow. They say it's because it could have been an accident, not because it could have been *not* an accident. Like nuts make their way into nut-free cafeterias all the time, like they could make their way onto a slice of pizza just as easily as they got into the cookies.

I know they won't give in on this, so I agree to pick up a sub or a wrap or something on my way into school and put it in the seriously 90's lunch tote Mom used to take with her to work. I'm allowed to drive myself tomorrow, at least. Because there aren't any nuts in my car, Dad jokes, when what he really means is that there aren't any Casey Everfelds in Centerville tomorrow. Like it's Casey who's the threat even though neither of my parents have said his name yet tonight. They haven't mentioned prom, either. I wonder if they think I've forgotten about it.

I tell them I'm going to bed early, that I really am tired. Lupus, you know. Because that's what it always used to be. I turn off the light in my room and lock the door, and they must think I'm asleep when they come upstairs and fight right down the hall. I think they've always assumed their bedroom door's soundproof. I guess I haven't given them a reason to think otherwise.

Their voices are loud tonight, those angry whispered shouts that aren't whispers at all. Sitting by my door, I can get some clear lines.

"Could stop her," comes from Mom.

They mean Casey, I know right away. But they're wrong about Casey. I stand up, not wanting to listen to any more.

I wish I could call him. I won't see him until tomorrow night, when he's back from the games and we're over at his place, and then it will be at least a little while before we'll be able to get away from Bimi and Nate. But this is just 24 hours. Not long, I tell myself, that this can't be a big deal, not talking to him for one day. A day's never felt this long to me before.

I'm finally lying down, wanting to dream of him again, when my mom's voice cuts through the wall. "We need to move," she says. It's clear, loud.

I sit up. There's some back and forth then, too fast for me to make out as I walk to my door, avoiding the creaky floorboards.

"It'll happen there, too," Dad says when his voice reaches its peak. And then I don't care how much noise I make crossing the room and getting back into bed. Maybe I don't want to know what they say next.

I'm thinking about Casey when I climb under the covers and close my eyes, but it's the bright room I dream of. I don't know why I feel dread this time when I look at

the wall in front of me. I could go through it, something
tells me—me. It has to be something inside of me saying
this. But I'm afraid of what's on the other side, of what *I'd
do* on the other side.

I stare at the wall until it fades into my usual umbrella
dream—the same boy without a face—and when I wake up
from that, the hallway's quiet.

In the morning, I don't call the umbrella dream a
nightmare, because it isn't one. It's comforting now,
familiar, like the dreams of Casey are even when I don't
recognize anything else in them.

And when I come downstairs and get my oatmeal,
anything left over from the room dream on my face my
mom just reads as stress. She assumes she's gotten what
she wants, that Casey and I are over and I'll be a sad third
wheel with Bimi and Nate at prom tomorrow, in a dress I
didn't pick out, with a random shaved spot at the back of
my head. Not exactly a night I'd want to remember.

I don't think about Casey not being at school today
until I'm halfway through my oatmeal. It makes it easy to
keep my face in sullen teenager mode.

Everything goes faster this morning since my parents
have decided I can drive again. Mom says because I seem

so much more steady now. She means because I'm so *not with Casey* now. Like Casey's been the threat all along, and my illness, the hit and run, my dreams, and everything else that stands in the way of whatever it is they think I'm supposed to be, of that *one day* they're always talking about, is one boy.

I think about this when I'm finally alone in my car. Maybe it's that teenage angst you're always hearing about and I'm learning to be a teenager, finally, trapped in my high school existence and being so short-sighted I think everything comes down to knowing, to being with, to loving one boy. But that's actually my parents, isn't it? *They're* the ones stuck on Casey, putting everything on him. At least I'm only obsessing on the good, on this pull I feel towards him in my head and in my body and how right everything is when he's with me.

I only have to not think about *why* he's with me, how this relationship came out of nowhere with a dream I had that came true. That feeling sits heavy in my stomach and leaves a tightness across my gut like all of me is stretching in some sort of everything-changing-at-once growth spurt. That's what I'm going to call it, a growth spurt. Not a freak upside downing of my entire existence that I know, somehow, is about to get faster. Because this—whatever it is, whatever's happening to me—still feels like a beginning.

Maybe the feeling in my stomach is why I go with a light chicken wrap instead of my usual greasy cheese sandwich when I get to the Sandwich Hut. I add a lot of lettuce and cucumbers and carrots like I'm going to push this worry out of my colon like that woman in the yogurt commercials says, like a normal bowel movement will make all of me normal again, *regular.* And like I *can* be normal again and the world can work normally with all the normal physical laws and high school social laws in place and I can still be with Casey.

When I get to the pool hallway, I swear it feels different without him, and I almost run into Nate when he meets me by the staircase. I can't concentrate on Bimi and her prom talk when she joins us. Tomorrow feels so far away now.

"Your mom's still..." Bimi gestures to my phone, glancing over her shoulder as some sophomores pass by us. We wait for the bell a little ways into the bathroom alcove today, away from the others.

"She still thinks I'm coming over tonight," I say. I try to smile then, to remember we've at least pulled this off, keeping a secret from my mom, and that I'll see Casey as soon as he's home from Salem.

"You have your lunch?" Bimi asks to keep me focused on something other than his not being here.

I point at my lunch tote over Nate's shoulder. I'll have to get better at focusing on him, on talking to him and acting right, since he's carrying everything for me all day. I should be acting *excited*, I guess, because of prom.

"And your hair, it's gonna be great," Bimi says. She found a style for me in some video blog, a neat twist that will cover the bald spot at the back of my head. And the salon where she made appointments for us is cheap and just a quick drive between our places tomorrow afternoon.

She grabs my arm when the bell rings, and I think she's going to say something else, something real, so I head her off.

"Tonight," I tell her. "I'll be better tonight."

She nods, and then she and Nate sandwich me between them for the walk to Econ.

I think I have a handle on this feeling by lunchtime. It's only a twinge in my stomach as I force down my wrap and a peach yogurt Mom must have put in her tote bag for me. That's supposed to look like love, I think, this quiet support of my gastrointestinal microflora.

I try to smile and nod along at Bimi and Nate as they talk about tomorrow. They think this will cheer me up. It should, but my head's not there.

I thought before that noticing Casey's absence was one

of those inevitable things, one of those just-can't-help-yourself things you read about in bad romance novels. But that's not what this is. This is like a cord between us I'm aware of all the time, but it's a tug I *want* to feel, one I'm trying to sustain, not one I want to break.

As Bimi and Nate walk with me to my car after Precalc, I tell them how well I am, that any hesitation they see in me today is just excitement—because I'm going to prom with Casey Everfeld tomorrow. And he'll be home in just a few hours with the team. This is what excitement is supposed to look like, I think, what new high school relationships probably always look like to other people.

I promise Nate I'll drive straight home, that he doesn't have to follow me. I almost do it, too, but my mom's at home, and I don't have the energy to put on my tragic teenager face again so soon. So I pass the house and drive around the park to the side lot where I met up with Casey the first time.

There are a bunch of people out today enjoying the nicer weather. I guess that's why I don't see Dave at first.

It's not like he sneaks up on me. It's not even like I'm afraid when he stops a few feet away, holding his hands up in front of his chest like he obviously expects me to be afraid of him.

It makes me angry, instead. I walk towards him before he even has a chance to come to me.

"I want to help you," Dave says.

And I'm even more surprised than he is, I think, when "fuck off" is what comes out of my mouth. I feel bad for this for just a second and almost apologize. But I don't. I guess I'm not sorry. I guess I'm less okay than I thought I was.

I stay where I am like I want to hear what he has to say to me, though, even if some part of me is sure I can't handle it.

I try to tell myself I *don't* know this, that I have no reason to believe this. Because what I should be thinking now is that Dave's just an overstepping youth pastor overzealous to save another high schooler who doesn't need saving from anything but him. Or myself. Or whatever it is that's getting to me in my sleep and turning my world upside down in all the ways I want.

Dave still has his hands up in front of him. I can't think of him as *Pastor* Dave now. I can't think of this as saving.

"We should talk," he says, gesturing to the bench a few feet away. The bench where I waited for Casey that first Saturday with him, where he found me when I didn't think he was coming. That feels like so long ago now.

I don't move. Dave doesn't, either. A kid on a bicycle

almost runs into him. There are so many people here. He can't hurt me with so many people here, I think. *I can't hurt him with so many people here*, some quiet voice in my head whispers, and then I really do have to sit down.

Dave comes around to stand in front of me. "I know what you're going through," he tells me then, like he could possibly know what I'm going through, like he could possibly know how this feels.

I wait. I guess I want him to say what I want to hear, that whatever's happening to me doesn't have anything to do with Casey. That it won't hurt him, at least.

"You said something about Casey," I say when I can't wait any longer. "In the parking lot."

"I'm sorry about that," Dave says, then, quickly, "about the parking lot."

A herd of power-walking women, their fists swinging at their boobs, parts around him like the Red Sea for Moses. I almost laugh at that, at how this makes me think of the Bible now like Dave really is a pastor and we're having some sort of a Come to Jesus moment on a beautiful spring day at the park.

He looks away, and I remind myself to breathe. This is just a tough conversation; soon, it will be over, and everything will go back to the way it was before. Never mind diving out of the way of cars or having my bike and my body mangled by a bumper or people going into anaphylaxis from cookies I was supposed to eat.

And I know there were no runaway cars or nutty cookies until I started dreaming of Casey Everfeld, until I started seeing numbers, until Casey Everfeld asked me out like this was the most natural thing in the world.

I swear Dave looks at every leaf on grass, avoiding my eyes. "I know you're having dreams," he says. "I know you're gearing up for something, and maybe you've gotten this from your parents, that you think you're *meant for* something."

Why is this when my heart starts pounding? Now, when we're in a crowd, when I don't have to run? When I can't run. I can't even move. It's the 'something.' My mom's word, always. My mom who's hiding things from me now, who's reading my texts like *I'm* the one who can't be trusted.

"Sam Rodriguez," I say. "The cookies. That should have been me."

Dave nods. "You're lucky it wasn't," he says. "But that's not going to be the end of it, Mischa. As long as you're still...as long as you're under the influence, these things, they'll keep happening. To you. To other people. It won't stop."

I open my mouth. But my tongue feels like it's too big, like I really did eat nuts. But it's not allergies or Dave. Maybe it was never him. Maybe it was always me doing this to myself and it was a chcoice. A choice I made selfishly, and one I still haven't told Casey about to give him a chance to make a different one.

"You won't be able to stop it on your own," Dave says. "I can't explain everything to you today, and you wouldn't understand it even if I did." He holds up a hand like he's going to stop me from interrupting, but I don't have anything to say.

"You have to stop the influence," he continues. "Just until we can figure out how to get everything under control. Until it's safe again. For you."

I don't move.

"For Casey, then," he says, meeting my eyes this time. "He didn't choose this."

It's Casey's name that keeps me here when Dave reaches into his pocket and pulls out a capsule. He sets it in his palm and holds it out to me.

"A pill," I say.

He nods. "Just one. That's all it takes."

"And everything will go back to normal," I say, "if I take that pill?"

"Everything will go back to normal," he confirms. "You take the pill, the influence goes away, and you start over."

"Start over?" Without Casey, he means, without any of this. They're a package deal.

"Exactly," Dave says, "and the power's gone."

"Whose power?" I ask, because it was influence before, like I was under the influence of someone else. I liked it better that way.

He doesn't respond.

"Not..." I can't say it. I can't swallow now, either.

"Yours," he says, after a second. "It's the...it's what's giving you the dreams."

And I knew this, didn't I, that *I'm* the one doing something, that I'm the one making things happen? I've chosen Casey on my own; I wasn't influenced in this.

"You just have to take one pill," Dave says.

I stand up, wishing I could tell him to fuck off again and forget this conversation ever happened.

But I think of Casey, instead, and I take the pill from Dave's hand, squeezing it in my fist as I run back to my car.

36

Casey

Greenville and Salem are easy wins. My fast balls come easy all day, and they're about all I throw.

We're up by a handful of runs by the last inning with Salem, and Greene lets Perkins pitch as he sits with me in the dugout and asks about my arm over and over. Because I'm throwing like a different person today, he says, throwing harder than we thought I'd ever be able to. I keep checking my watch. We should be home about an hour before Mischa and Bimi come over.

When the game finally ends 7-2, the guys are all loud, and they stay pumped as we change out. Perkins can't stop grinning and thanking me over and over like I was the one throwing for him. Because he doesn't get that this isn't generosity, isn't humility, my letting him pitch. This is him needing to be ready when I'm not there for state.

I have trouble answering him when he starts talking about working on his slider next week, and I get away a while before the team gets on the bus. Ellen and Rick have already pulled up the Lincoln Rick says he'll have washed tomorrow before prom. For Nate for prom, since I don't want to ride with him and Bimi. It still has the dealer sticker in the window. Ellen will make him scrape off the tape so it doesn't show in the pictures.

She fusses over the air conditioning when I get in. It's that sticky kind of hot today, and she blasts the vents back at me, chattering about the game and telling me I should rest up. I'll be up late tonight with Mischa over, and then tomorrow with prom.

So I try to sleep, thinking of my first foster parents telling us Christmas would come sooner if we went to bed early. It works; Christmas is just different now, I think as I picture Mischa and will the Lincoln to fly faster down 71 back to Centerville.

When I wake up, we've stopped. I sit up. Rick's standing at a gas pump that's already clicked off, and Ellen's just behind him. They see me at the same time and stop talking.

She gets in then but doesn't say anything.

"What is it?" I ask.

"The car," she says.

"The car?" I look out at Rick. He's gone to a trash can by the station. He wipes his hands with a paper towel and avoids my eyes when he comes back and gets in the driver's seat.

"A light," Ellen tells me. "It's a light that came on in the dash. Something with the engine."

I almost ask about the light. Instead, I ask how far away we are from home.

"A couple hours."

"An hour and a half," Rick says at the same time.

She looks at him. They're fighting again.

I don't ask if we can keep going. I don't want to give them the idea that we might not.

Rick pulls across the street to a little motel and gets out without saying anything else.

"Just until we can get someone to look at the car," Ellen says, glancing at me in the rearview.

I ask questions for a while. I even try to look at whatever's wrong with the engine myself, but she won't pop the hood. Rick's inside calling a mechanic, so I walk around the motel a few times with my phone, writing all of this in a text to Nate, about how I thought we'd be early and now we might be late and I need him to get this message to Mischa through Bimi.

"This won't take long," Ellen tells me when I get back in the car. "You need to relax."

"Three hours," I say. "They're coming in three hours."

"I know," she says. "It'll be fine." But now she won't look at me, either.

37

Mischa

I check my glove compartment twice, at the light on seventh and again at the stop sign on Wilson, where I turn onto Hillcrest, like the pill might get loose and go somewhere on its own. When I was getting ready, I must have opened and closed the jewelry box I'd put it in a dozen times. Then I suffocated it in a cocoon of tissues and shoved it into the corner of my glove box. Because I'm a teenager, and when you leave pills in your room, your parents think you're on pills, right? And now I really am one of those teenagers who has a pill I shouldn't have. Or that I should have. Probably that I should have.

The Everfelds' house is dark when I pull up to the curb, and I get out the pill one more time, unwrap the tissues and look at it again. It's just a capsule with white powder inside. Dave never called it medicine, did he?

I'll take it after prom. That's the deal I made in my head, like that I'll tell Casey everything after prom. Because I would have told him sooner, the night of the accident, if I hadn't been hit. I should have told him when I woke up. But what's another day now? And I guess then I won't have to tell him because the pill will undo whatever it is he's gotten caught up in, and then it will be over and at least he'll be safe.

And what will I be? *Starting over*, whatever Dave means by that, without this power or whatever it is—not something I asked for, but something I know I won't give up on my own.

I shake off tomorrow when I get to the Everfelds' front door, to this part of my life that isn't really mine, that Casey didn't choose like I chose him.

It takes a second for the door to open after I ring the bell. It's Nate who opens it. Not Casey. And I know right away he's not here. Neither are Rick and Ellen, Nate tells me.

"You should come in," he says, stepping back and opening the door wider.

I shake my head.

"Casey's not...I think there might be something wrong with his phone," Nate says.

"Can you have Bimi text me?" I ask.

"Come in," he repeats, gesturing to the living room. "The game probably just ran late. They'll be back soon. I ordered pizza. Let me get you a drink."

But my feet don't move. "No," I say, even as I try to tell myself everything really is okay, that Casey will be home soon. That maybe he's just going through a patch without a cell signal or his phone ran out of battery.

"Can you have Bimi text me?" I repeat, because these are the only words that seem to want to come out of me now. "If they—if Casey gets home. When Casey gets home, I mean, have Bimi text me?"

Nate's nearly hidden behind the door that's all the way open now, trying to coax me inside like a scared cat.

"She'll be here soon," he tells me. "She said a few minutes ago she was…"

"Just have her text me that you two are caught out somewhere and she's not home yet," I say. "I told my mom I was at her place."

Nate finally agrees, but I recognize his car following me all the way to Magnolia, I guess because he can see I'm not as okay as I keep saying I am.

I have my face under control—I swear I do. I stayed outside the garage for like twenty minutes just trying not to cry—by the time I come inside.

"Honey?" Mom says right as I open the door, before she even sees me. She sounds bad; it's one of those gut-dropping, voice-cracking questions right before the killer gets you in a low budget horror film, that *Is someone there?* moment. Maybe she can smell it on me, some hormone teenagers produce when we're about to fall apart. I guess this smell is new on me.

I almost run into her at the kitchen.

"What's wrong?" she asks.

I try to blow by her. Like a teenager, you know. "Nothing," I say.

"Honey." She follows me to the stairs.

"I'm fine." I don't turn around. "Bimi's just out with Nate. She'll text later." One, two, three steps. There are only eight more. My bedroom feels so much farther tonight, my feet almost as heavy as they were on the Everfelds' front step when Nate opened the door instead of Casey.

My mom's behind me when I get to my room.

"What?" I ask.

"You tell me," she says.

And I almost *do* tell her. Something, anyway. That Bimi and I had a fight. That I got a bad grade on a test that just posted. Some other lie. But I shouldn't have to lie to my mother for her own sake.

"Can I not just be okay?" I ask, when what I mean is can I not be a freaking—a *fucking* teenager—who's just not fucking anyone? Can I not go up to my room on a Friday night nervous about going to prom alone tomorrow or so vain I can't deal with the chunk of hair I'm missing at the back of my head or worried about the scar on my forehead not getting covered by my concealer? Is that so much to ask?

But it is. Because I'm not a fucking teenager. Or I wasn't, before. I didn't build up a baseline in this range. Instead, I was perpetually undramatic Mischa Kenning-Elliott of the perpetually quiet Friday nights. Like this one should be, with Casey. My last Friday night with Casey.

"I don't want you here," I say when Mom follows me into my room.

"I know that," she says. She sits down on the corner of my bed anyway.

I go stand by my closet. The pill's at the bottom of my purse now under a pack of mints. But she's not looking at my purse. It's not like she's ever had a reason to go through it before.

She doesn't say anything right away, and I wonder if this is when I call her out on reading my texts or when she calls me out on lying to her. I don't know how this works, the lying thing. One of us should be calling the other out, though, I'm pretty sure. One of us should be yelling. It feels like I should be the one yelling.

"Would you tell me what's on your mind?" she asks, instead.

I try to think of what I can tell her when everything true feels off the table.

"Please," she says.

The truth is that Casey's still on my mind. And Casey will be on my mind, I know, until I take this pill after prom tomorrow—I guess at midnight, to really get this night, like Cinderella. I wish I could laugh at how ridiculous it is that I'm living the wrong part of the fairy tale I never wanted. Even as a little girl, I wasn't into Prince Charming, wasn't into changing.

My mom's looking at me like she can see through me. So I try to convince her I'm the healthy kind of teenage crazy, the kind of teenage crazy I should have been sometime before now. I tell her this is prom drama because I have the same dress as Kaitlen Miller, and I say it like *this* is the end of my world.

She doesn't buy it. So I turn away, sit down at my laptop and wake it up. My thesis loads on the screen.

"I'm going to work on my paper," I say, mostly to the computer. "Until I hear from Bimi, anyway. And don't say

I'm stressed."

"I wasn't."

Then she's quiet, and I don't have a choice but to turn around. "I'm sorry," I say as soon as I see her face. Because whatever I've said—however much of a fucking teenager I am right now—I actually think I can't be as miserable as my mother looks. She looks worse than you do the night before prom when the boyfriend you're lying to your parents about isn't home when he should be and you have the same dress as the head cheerleader and a chunk of hair missing and a scar on your forehead you don't think your concealer will hide.

"I...I have to show you something," Mom says.

I go sit by her on the bed. She doesn't look at me as she gets out her phone.

"I don't want to," she adds. But she holds out the phone anyway and scrolls through a series of pictures.

I don't recognize Casey in the first one. I do recognize Kaitlen Miller. The second's just the back of her head, and I still almost don't recognize Casey. It's his face. It's that it's not his face, or at least it's not a face I associate with him.

In the third picture, Kaitlen's pressed up against him, and they look like they're going to kiss. But there's something wrong with this thought, I tell myself right away. It's from too many stupid vampire books in our school library, the kind that can make love look like violence and possession. This is seriously toxic, I want to scream, because of course I want to think about shitty depictions of romance or anything, really, but Casey and Kaitlen Miller and how he doesn't look in this picture how he looked when he was about to kiss me. He doesn't look how he's *ever* looked with me.

This is passion, my mom wants to tell me. This is what it looks like. She just says it with an, "I'm sorry you had to see that."

But she's wrong. I know this, at least. I put down those books and grew out of that idea of love a long time ago.

Only I'm still staring at her phone, at the last picture, when she pulls it away. It takes me a second to remember I shouldn't be staring at these photos; I told her Casey and I aren't a thing anymore. But I guess she can see I'm full of shit now, too.

And maybe it doesn't matter. Maybe this is the game, my knowing she's spying on me and her knowing I'm lying about Casey.

I don't manage to say anything quickly enough, so she has a chance to keep going. "I know you're disappointed," she says. "I know you thought...I know you thought that this wasn't some sort of a joke, him asking you to prom, but that's certainly what..."

"It doesn't matter." I'm surprised by how steady my voice comes out.

Mom finally looks at me. She opens her mouth, and I wonder if we're going to tell each other the truth now.

"I'm fine," I tell her, instead.

"Practical jokes like this..." Mom says, because I guess she's not finished, that she's not sure I'm fully off Casey yet. Maybe longing makes some other teenager smell she can detect. Maybe love does.

"No," I say. Because even at my most insecure, I can't think of this is as a practical joke, Casey asking me to prom. Whatever a *practical* joke is. That's something my mom would know about, I tell myself, not something I'd know. Not something Casey would do. But that's not how I have to finish this. "I'm fine," I say. "I mean it. I don't care."

And maybe she believes me. She leaves, finally, a few minutes later, and it's not until I'm lying awake at two in the morning after three texts from Bimi, the last one around midnight saying she's still "out with Nate," that I finally wonder how the fuck my mom got those photos.

That night in my dream, I face the wall. I can see myself in a reflection from its surface as I walk towards it

—confidently this time, like I know what I'm going to do. I don't recognize myself right away in the reflection. I don't look like me.

This time, the wall opens as soon as I get to it. The room in front of me then is even more foreign than the last. That one's disappeared, the wall solid again behind me. This space is larger and has a window, the shimmer of the walls broken by blackness outside and a line of screens.

I walk to the window, and at first, I think what I see through it is a blue-green marble with white swirls over its surface. It takes me a second to recognize it—*Earth.*

I watch it for a while before I feel like I need to do something—something big, something I've been waiting to do for a long time, and I lift my hand to one of the screens.

But this is voluntary, I know as I watch my fingers move, gesturing over the screen like I'm conducting some inaudible symphony. I know what I'm doing right up until I wake up covered in sweat.

When I roll over, the sheets stick to my legs, and it takes a second for my eyes to adjust enough to make out the red letters on my alarm clock. It's just past three in the morning.

I cross the room and get my phone. I left it plugged in thinking I wouldn't keep checking it if I couldn't reach it from the bed. My heart's pounding, and I look out my window like maybe something different will be outside it now, like maybe I could soar through this wall, too, and be somewhere else.

There aren't any texts from Nate or Bimi, and I can't wait to hear from Casey any longer.

Can we be friends? I write him, since I don't know what else to say that my mom could read before tonight. My last *tonight* with Casey.

I watch for the dots that say he's typing, but nothing comes. My phone keeps going black. My heart keeps pounding. But maybe that's just prom, because after all, I am seventeen, and for all I know, these nerves might be normal when you're lying to your parents and your date's gone AWOL. Like junior prom dates do, I tell myself when I look at my reflection in the mirror, trying to believe this. But I don't look like somebody you'd believe now.

There are sixteen hours before the dance. Before he'll be there, I tell myself, this time out loud. I repeat it over and over as I try to remember the getting ready schedule Bimi and I talked about, or at least that Bimi talked about. I think we were supposed to bathe in cucumbers or something last night.

Around five, I settle on a shower, trying to scrub off my scalp with my fingernails. I wash my hair twice and accidentally open a scab where my stitches are dissolving in the back. The blood rinses away in foamy pink water, and I imagine this feeling washing away with it.

The bathroom's steamy, and I trip over the toilet trying to get to my phone when it beeps. But it's just another text from Bimi asking if I'm all right.

I tell her I am, like typing it will make me believe it, and wrap up in a towel to pad back to my room. I sit down at my computer and open my thesis document then, reading through it out loud to give myself something else to focus on.

I can hear the syllables, but they're just noises; I can't seem to process them, to think of anything but Casey. It's like we're connected by strings that only feel tight when there's something wrong, that pull that comes from whatever Dave says is bad but that's never *felt* bad. It's an ache now, deep and dull and overwhelming at once, like it's growing too big inside me and is going to push all the tears out of my body. Like it might push *me* out of my body. And I guess in the end, it will.

38

Casey

I pace around the motel room Saturday morning after breakfast. The car should be ready. We should be home.

"We're just a couple hours away," Ellen reminds me as I stop to pick up my phone where it's plugged in on the dresser. "There's still plenty of time."

"The pastor," I tell her, because I don't know how else to say this, and I can't stop thinking it.

"What?"

"The pastor. Dave. He's not...there's something wrong with him," I say. "I need to be there."

Ellen tries to calm me down then without looking at me. She says it was just a bad dream I had. I didn't sleep well. I didn't sleep at all, she means.

"No," I tell her. "I have to get back."

"In just a little while," she says. "It wasn't easy getting a mechanic out to the middle of nowhere, and what is this about the pastor?"

I try to tell her, but it doesn't sound any less crazy when I explain it, about how Dave's not a pastor, or at least that's not why he's here. About Mischa and how I know she's in danger even if I don't know why.

Ellen steps over the blanket I kicked on the floor last night and sits on the edge of that mattress.

"We have to go," I repeat as I zip up my bag and look out the window. "Is Rick..."

"On his way," she says, but she doesn't stand up.

So I grab my bag and go outside. I swear the sun hurts then. I should have brought a hat. But that doesn't matter; all I keep seeing, now in splotches of yellow sun spots, is Dave Parker's face.

It takes me a while squinting into the sun to make out the Lincoln at the service station whose parking lot is separated from the motel by some grass, and I head that way, pulling my phone from my pocket.

There's still no response from Nate from last night. Ellen said over and over that he was fine, that everything was fine. But Nate's never not texted me back before.

So I don't have a choice but to text Mischa something her mom could read, something that goes along with this lie about us not going to prom together. It takes me too long to come up with it. I keep stubbing my toes into the grass.

I settle on, *I won't be with Nate at the beginning tonight if you want to do the before prom stuff with Bimi.* Then I tell her I'm sorry about everything and hope this is enough.

39

Mischa

I'm still in my pajamas sitting at my computer when my mom knocks on my door. The pill's balanced between the *h* and the *y* on my keyboard now. It's strange, I think as I slide it behind the monitor, that this is the first time in seventeen years I've had to make a decision that wasn't just for me.

I put on my blank teenager face, and my voice doesn't give anything away when I tell Mom to come in.

But she doesn't make the same effort. She looks like she feels sorry for me, and her face is so rough it would almost make me feel sorry for myself if it didn't make me so angry, instead. But I guess this is how the anger's supposed to come out, isn't it, at my mom, instead of at myself? Or at the occult, as Kaitlen Miller would put it. The idea that I'm possessed or under the influence of dark forces or whatever Kaitlen imagines would make me at least smile any other day.

Mom has ice cream with her this time, a tub of those little chocolate-covered nuggets of thick vanilla cream I used to gorge on in middle school with Bimi when we'd stay up late together watching movies on the weekends. I haven't had them in a while.

I must look like I need them now. Mom holds out the tub to me as she walks to my bed.

I take it and sit beside her, trying to keep my face still.

"You should text Bimi," she says when the third ice cream nugget—fudge coating, my favorite—is melting on my tongue.

I look up.

"You said you were meeting her for a hair appointment, didn't you?"

It takes me a second to swallow. So my mom doesn't think I'm going to prom at all. And then it's just acid in the back of my throat, anger. I don't want to hate her today, but I know, as I reach into the tub and force myself to put another piece of ice cream in my mouth, that I've never hated my mother like I hate her now. I think I've never hated *anyone* like I hate her now.

"Right," I say, looking down into the tub.

She strokes my hair, drying now, frizzy. I focus on counting the pieces of the ice cream left in the tub. Before I've even gotten past the top layer, my eyes blur like the chocolate coating that's melting along the sides of the carton as the nuggets soften into each other.

"This is for the best," Mom says, then, "you have so much ahead of you."

I swallow. Who knew ice cream could stick in your throat?

"And there's always next year for prom."

Then I'm crying, *really* crying, and there's nothing I can do to stop it. My mom wraps her arms around me and rocks me like she used to when I was a little girl, when I cried over the kind of things that ice cream nuggets could make better.

I wonder if this is how hate feels. How I hate her for being the reason I have to lie to her. How I hate that she can't comfort me now. How I hate that she's turned me into a liar like she is. But I know this isn't only hate; this is loss, too, because somehow I'm sure, however we got here, that this is the last time I will sit on my bed with a carton of ice cream nuggets and my mom rocking me while I cry.

I try to stop this thought, try to listen to her like I can believe what she says. I tell myself everything will be all right, that things aren't as bad as they seem. I almost manage to shame myself out of these tears, too, knowing no amount of makeup will cover the redness they leave behind or the way my face swells.

And I wonder if my mom's right and I shouldn't be going to prom at all as I cry myself to sleep and dream of the umbrella again.

40

Casey

I swear my phone's broken when I get out of the shower. Time hasn't moved. The bathroom didn't even steam up.

An hour, Rick told me. That was only seven minutes ago, when he said I should go back to the hotel and wait in the air conditioning so I wouldn't get sweaty.

Just a little longer, Ellen said when I came in, and shouldn't I just shower here, if I was so worried about being ready for tonight? So I'll be clean when we get home, so getting dressed won't take me so long.

But now I've showered and no time's passed. We're waiting on something with the car that Rick said was complicated, something with the electrical system. Not something I should worry about, Ellen keeps saying, that there's still so much time before the dance.

I almost hit her with the bathroom door when I open it.

"Sorry," I say at the same time she does, but she's still not meeting my eyes. She says something about the hotel shampoo as she passes by me and shuts the door behind her.

I wait until I hear her turn on the shower to plug my phone in on the dresser again. It's been losing charge a lot. I scroll through my text messages with Nate all the way back to Thursday, when I saw Mischa last, and it feels like this wasn't just the day before yesterday.

I sit in the hard chair by the window with my phone in my hand and tell myself I can wait, that I can watch the minutes of this hour pass by, that I can count seconds if I have to. That I can safely do anything with my head but what I'm doing now, letting it run away with me.

I don't know why it takes me so long to think of Bimi. Bimi, whose parents don't read her texts. Or at least I don't think they do. I start with something safe to be sure.

I haven't heard from Nate, I tell her.

The dots flash right away to say she's typing. Or right away in real time. In my time, these seconds take forever.

You didn't write him back last night, she says, then, before I can process this—I guess time can change, can go too fast, too—*Where are you?*

I look at the door to the bathroom, then back at my

phone. There's still nothing there from Nate. Just like there's nothing from Mischa.

Ellen. She must have blocked me from Nate's phone. And she didn't tell him where we were. Last night, she said she'd explained everything.

I take a breath, or I try to. My lungs are too tight, like that time they thought I had asthma in eighth grade, when Ellen dragged me to three different pulmonologists even once we knew it was just the pollen and the allergy medicine was working.

I don't see the other text right away. *Mischa either*, Bimi says.

And that's when I see yellow satin drenched in blood.

I'm out the door before I can text Bimi back.

41

Mischa

When I wake up from my nap, all I can think of to text Bimi—I guess I'm really just texting my mom now—is *Not coming tonight. Have fun.*

Mom's waiting for me in the kitchen when I get downstairs. She's still looking at me like she feels sorry for me. Not like she's sorry for lying to me, though, for spying on me. Not like she's sorry for the pictures. The pictures she took, I wonder? But there's no sense in wondering this; it doesn't matter now.

What matters is that I still look miserable and that she can't tell one kind of misery from another. What matters is that I don't have to act when I show her how hurt I am and that I ignore the phone on my bed that won't stop ringing— Bimi every time. I can hear it all the way from down here.

Mom watches as I pull out another container of ice cream nuggets from behind some frozen blueberries. She knew this was coming, or she wouldn't have gotten them. And I figure if my world is crashing down around me and everything that matters to me is going away in a handful of hours, I may as well have a second fucking tub of ice cream.

I stare at my phone for a while after I go back upstairs, at all the messages from Bimi I can't answer. There's no way to tell her I really am coming tonight, but I've made up my mind. However I have to do it, maybe hurling ice cream nuggets behind me at my parents like fudgy bullets. Maybe through the window with my bedroom door locked. Maybe in these pajamas that are dotted with chocolate after an afternoon of being every bit the miserable teenager my mom expects to see in them.

So I don't have to fake any angst when I hear Mom talking to her at the front door a little after four.

"Nate texted me," Bimi says first thing when I come down. She looks pointedly at me.

"Nate," I say, and have to bite the sides of my lips. *Casey.* Casey texted her. I try to breathe, try to keep my face still, my body still.

"He was worried about you, too, when you weren't

answering your phone."

"I'm okay," I tell her. I roll my eyes back towards the kitchen, where I know my mom's listening. "I'm just...I'm not ready to do tonight."

Bimi nods. But Bimi is Bimi, and no one would believe a Bimi who gave up so easily. So she doesn't. And since it's not possible to overplay a Bimi disappointment, she really does it justice. She whines. She pouts. She stomps her foot. Finally, she feigns exasperation, sighing enough times in a row that she sounds like those monks we watched a video of in Mr. Martin's class doing their shamanistic breathing.

"I'll see you later," I tell her when she's finished. "At school Monday." And I don't know why once it's out of my mouth, I'm not sure if this is true. Maybe when I start over, I really do start over. Maybe there's no more school, no more thesis, no more Bimi.

She winks and lets out one last huff before she goes to her car.

Then I put my angsty face back on as I pass my mom and stomp—really stomp—up the stairs to my room. But all that matters now is that Casey texted Bimi and I know he's okay. He'll be there.

42

Casey

Ellen's still in the shower when I run outside. I let the door slam shut behind me and don't wait to find out if Ellen hears it. She can't stop me anymore.

Rick must see me running through the lawn towards the highway. There are enough cars; somebody will pick me up. But it's his voice yelling that he can help that makes me double back towards the service station.

"Mischa," I say, out of breath when he meets me at the edge of the asphalt.

Rick nods. "Mischa," he says, and then he holds out his hand with the keys to the Lincoln.

"The car? It's okay?" I ask.

"Take it," he says.

My arm won't reach out right away. Because this is wrong. Not the car, like they've been saying since last night. This is something bigger.

"I'm sorry," Rick says, but he's looking at the keys. Not at me. Like Ellen won't look at me now. Because they're both full of shit, and I want to scream this, to confront them. *Do they have something to do with blood on a yellow dress?* my head asks. But I shake this away. There won't be any blood on a yellow dress, I tell myself again. I'll get there.

"The car's okay?" I repeat.

Rick looks over my shoulder, then finally meets my eyes. "You can't keep it long," he says. "We'll be able to find it by the plate."

It's the *we* that keeps me here.

"You saw something with Mischa," he says.

I don't ask how he knows this. It doesn't matter now. I take the keys.

Rick's looking at the motel. I turn to look at it, too. But Ellen's still inside, and my phone's quiet; she doesn't know I'm gone yet.

Maybe Rick can read my mind. "Give me your phone," he says.

I look back at him.

"She can track your phone. Ellen. I'm sorry," he says. "We were...it was a mistake interfering."

"Interfering?" I ask, but I don't wait for an answer before I give him the phone. He pockets it.

I'm running out of time. I know this. *No more Rick,* my

head says.

I follow him around the side of the station where the Lincoln's parked. He's moving faster than I've seen him move before, faster than he moved when he used to throw with me trying to keep the ball from landing in Mrs. Arnold's petunias next door. *No more Mrs. Arnold's petunias*, my head says as I press the key fob to unlock the car.

Rick has his wallet out when I'm about to close the door behind me. "Take it," he says, "It'll buy you time."

So I do, and then I'm gone.

43

Mischa

Restless. I am *restless*. And this is what I can't get out of my head. I spell it over and over like the SAT words I had trouble remembering—I guess those don't matter anymore, either—typing it with my fingers on my knee as I wait in my room. I wouldn't call this a panic attack. Or maybe I would; maybe this is what panic looks like in someone like me, like sneaking out to prom, like taking a pill, like wanting so badly not to.

I know it isn't just that, though. I know, even if I can't make sense of any of the other things I see when I go to sleep, and now sometimes when I only close my eyes, that everything changes tonight. This is more than sneaking out to prom. This is more than a pill, more than starting over.

It feels like I've been sitting on my bed for forever when I hear my parents fighting downstairs. My mom's voice is sharp, and it cuts through the walls. It doesn't go on long this time before I see Dad's car driving away from my window, and I'm still in my pajamas when Mom texts me to say she's going out for a few hours if I'm okay.

I'm perfectly fine, I write her back right away. A seventeen-year-old fine, you know, an in-for-prom-night-grieving-an-AWOL-boyfriend fine.

I wait until she's pulled out of the garage to shimmy into my dress and do my hair—in just a ponytail, because I don't know how else to hide the bald spot at the back of my head by myself.

And thinking of Casey is enough that my hair doesn't matter, or the foundation I can't get to settle over the scar on my forehead. I'm already running late, but at least this isn't a going out a window and rappelling from the roof with my shawl situation. And that's what I'm thinking about, anything but the pill nestled in tissues in my bra, when I drive out into the darkness.

I hit three green lights in a row, so the drive to school doesn't take as long as it should. Or maybe it just feels shorter tonight, like everything else that's happening so quickly. I imagine tonight will fly by and I'll wonder later, when I take the pill, if it really happened, if I really got to have this night first.

I decide when I find a parking spot—right away, the first row in front of the gym—not to think about later. I leave my phone off, and as I'm touching up my lipstick in the rearview mirror, I try not to think about how Casey and I won't have a chance to do the *you look so nice*'s with each other or pose for pictures in front of flowerbeds, maybe in front of Mrs. Phillips' roses that would look so right, so cheerful next to this yellow satin. I don't think about how I won't be able to pin a boutonniere on his jacket—Bimi was going to pick one up for me—or fuss over a wrist corsage like I should be tonight.

Just tonight, just a few more hours to even be in this dress, to be with Casey, to be the *me* I've been these last weeks.

Something flashes behind my eyes when I open my car door. I see a field and a house, another place I don't know. I'm still not sure where some of these flashes come from. They're like the dreams, only I'm awake. But these will be gone in just a handful of hours, too.

So I stand up, my heels clicking on the sidewalk as I pull my wrap tighter around my shoulders. Black light from the dance floor puddles in a hazy streak of purple around me when I get to the gym door, the breeze whistling in my ears, and I tell myself I can do this, that these next steps aren't as big as they feel.

44

Casey

I thought I'd be messed up now. Shaking, sweating—*thinking*, at least, about Ellen or about something Rick said, trying to make sense of it. They obviously know more than they're telling me. I didn't think I'd be able to get dressed in the few minutes I took at the house or that I'd be passing for normal in front of all the chaperones, all the smiling parents who don't know what's coming.

I block out the chatter, the strobe lights, and the music from the dance floor as I watch the parking lot through the stained glass bulldog.

Bimi and Nate are hovering somewhere behind me. They say they're *not* hovering every time I tell them they are. Bimi keeps texting and reports about every two minutes that Mischa's phone must be off. She's sure that's all it is, she tells me, but she doesn't sound sure. I look back at her when she says it this time. She looks nervous. Because she's just buying time, like I am. Like Rick told me to. I don't know how much of it we have.

I see the headlights of another car and know it's Mischa before I catch a glimpse of her dress—yellow. I can tell even through the brown paw of the bulldog. She's glowing. *Like a target*, my head says. Then I'm down the hallway and running to the side doors of the gym with Bimi and Nate trying to keep up behind me.

I catch her just as she's walking in, and she lets me pull her all the way across the dance floor, weaving between the bodies gathered in circles yelling "Shout!" with the music. We catch it just right, passing through when everybody's up with their arms in the air, and I almost do a double take when I sideswipe Kaitlen Miller as we round the corner by the bathrooms. It's the same flash of yellow satin, the same dress Mischa's wearing with a matching wrap.

I look back at Mischa like there's some chance I might have grabbed the wrong girl, but she's laughing, and we get away before we can hear what I'm sure will be a classic Kaitlen Miller meltdown.

We don't slow down until we're around the corner of the kitchens. The music doesn't reach here, and all of a sudden, it's so quiet that I can hear my breath, her breath. She runs into me when I stop by the big refrigerators.

I try to slow down my heart then, to slow down everything and feel her here beside me in the darkness. Solid Mischa. Solid yellow satin that I can't really see now, but at least that isn't covered in blood.

I try to tell her this, about what was just a bad dream, even though I wasn't asleep, try to apologize and explain about Ellen and Rick and everything else I don't understand yet. I even try to tell her how beautiful she looks, since I'm sure she does. It all pours out at once like I'll only have this one chance to say it.

45

Dave Parker—that's not his name, but it's the name of the pastor he took on when he had to, *because* he had to—lost sight of Mischa for a minute, but he has her back now.

It takes too long, he thinks, to line up the shot. He's practiced. Pretty much his whole life has been getting ready for this shot.

It was so easy to do everything that came before it. To find her. To give her the pill. The pill she won't take, he knows, and since the nuts and the cars failed, too, it comes down to him now, to this shot.

It was easy getting into the gym, sneaking up the staircase to the balcony where he could set up behind some glittery curtains. No one was paying attention to the chaperones, and he had a name tag on when he came in the band door, one of those standard ones with a blue border and a *Hello*.

No one sees the barrel of his gun poking through the curtains, and when he finally pulls the trigger, he knows he's hit her before she falls.

46

Mischa

I thought Casey pulled me, but maybe we both started running at the same time. Maybe I even knew what I'd see when we passed the dance floor, when I caught a glimpse of yellow satin puddled on the basketball court and soaked through with blood.

Casey tugs me around the corner that leads to the pool hall. When I blink, I see Kaitlen, yellow satin and blood again. Blood that should have been mine.

So I guess I'm not surprised when I see Dave barreling towards us. Shouldn't this be surprise? But I don't have time to wonder. Not now.

These hallways echo, shiny white concrete blocks that are all shadows tonight.

I yank off my heel and throw it behind me into the darkness. I hear it land, but he could still be that close.

Casey has my other hand and is pulling me forward. He catches my shoulder when we skid around the corner of the gym.

"Here," he says, "the stairs."

My feet are slippery now, starting to sweat. I squeeze his hand and balance against his weight when I don't catch the railing right away. I count the stairs then—*Five. Six. Seven.* That's better, isn't it, to count than to think about blood soaking through buttery yellow satin? *Eleven. Twelve.*

There's a loud creak, and Casey pushes me through the door to the boys' locker room. He leads me blindly then between the rows of metal mesh and through the showers. There's a high window at the back, the moonlight shimmering through the frosted glass.

As I climb up onto the ledge, my foot gets caught in my dress, and I feel the satin pull around my hips, but my breathing's too loud to hear the tear.

My hands touch the glass, and then Casey's there beside me pushing at the hinges. When I slide my head under the frame, he shoves me forward.

On the other side, a wall of hot air hits me before I can stand up, the dew creeping through the fabric over my knees.

Then we're running again, across the lawn and through

the baseball diamond, my feet sucking down into the clipped grass. We don't stop to close the window. We don't look back.

The only lights now are far away, out on Fifth Street, but I imagine I can hear something behind us, that there's more noise beyond my breath and our feet and the swoosh of satin as it gets caught up between my legs.

"You're okay?" Casey asks when we get to the other side of the field, to the chain link fence there.

Once we're still, I can hear the buzzing of the cicadas, can feel the moisture in the air squeezing my lungs and sticking my dress to me.

"The woods," I tell him, and this is when it hits me that I won't be able to come back to these woods, to the fallen tree where I used to sit on warm afternoons to study with the sun shaking down through the leaves. That's gone for me now. Everything I know will be gone soon.

I hear water running through the irrigation ditch below the fence, but I can't see the bottom of it. I squint down into the darkness as I climb, the chain link digging into my feet.

Somewhere behind us, there's a scream.

Casey jumps down. When I get to the top, all I can see are his hands reaching up out of the darkness.

But I know he's going to catch me, the way I know him

beyond reason, beyond explanation.

"Just fall," he says.

And I do.

He catches me, his arms around my waist, his breath warm in my ear, and I realize I'm not scared anymore. Not scared as the sirens pick up. Not scared as we race deeper into the woods, my feet sucking down into the mud. Not scared of whatever comes next, as long as I have his hand.

We don't stop until we're almost to the senior lot. "The car," he says, and points ahead. He parked in the corner that drops off into a ditch like he knew this was coming.

We make a run for it. Maybe we both knew we'd be running tonight.

I don't look back as I grab the handle of the passenger door. As Casey gets his door open and the lights come on inside, the paper in the window seems to glow, and that's when I see it clearly for the first time. It's the car that hit me.

I open my mouth, but nothing comes out.

Casey's saying something, but by then, I'm running again.

47

Casey

Mischa's halfway across the woods now. I keep pace a few yards behind her and let her run.

I wait until she's slowed down to say her name again. She stops when she hears my voice this time and turns to look at me, but I can't see her face. She's just a silhouette against the lights over the stadium they've turned on now, looking for Dave. From me. *She's running from me.*

"The Lincoln. It's the car that hit you," I say, and of course now I know this. Now, when it's too late. It feels like my voice goes too far, though, that it goes right through her.

Mischa doesn't move.

"It's Rick's." I don't say I wasn't the one who hit her, like Ellen must have really been asking me before. Because I would never have hit her. She has to know this. I can't convince her if she doesn't.

She looks over her shoulder. The police have already blocked off the entrances to the complex.

"Rick told me to go. He gave me the car. He didn't tell me..." How do you say *that he tried to kill you first?* Even if he just lent Dave the Lincoln. Or somebody. That's what he said, isn't it, that he lent it out to somebody and they put a dent in it? But he knew. He had to know.

I wait. There's nothing else I can say now, when we have to go. Because we haven't bought that much time. That's what Rick told me this was, taking the car, just buying time, and I don't think he was lying to me then.

As I watch the shadow that's Mischa, I feel like there's something shaking in the center of my body, like I'm going to explode. Like anything could set this off. Like her walking away from me now will.

Finally, she takes a step towards me.

48

Mischa

The lot with the Lincoln—I don't think about it as the car that hit me anymore, don't flash to the papers in the window—and the lane out to Fifth Street are swarmed by police now. We watch through some branches as an ambulance pulls away under the big bulldog.

I squeeze Casey's hand just to feel that he's here. It feels like that's all that matters now.

Just now. There's not a later, I know, for very long. Just like there's nowhere for us to go, no *us* at all, my head keeps reminding me, after tonight.

I dreamed of prom being quiet, of spinning in slow circles lost in a sweet purple twilight until our time really did run out. I told myself I'd enjoy this, even if I know it's wrong, until midnight. That's when I decided, midnight, like Cinderella. I can't get it out of my head.

Now we won't be able to get away. The police blocked off the rest of the complex as soon as they'd covered all the entrances to the gym.

A little while ago, we saw my parents pull into the teachers' lot, and there's a crowd gathered there now waiting for news.

I hold my breath as an officer with a megaphone addresses them—*One victim. Condition unknown. Parents already contacted.*

The ambulance had lights and sirens; she must have still been alive. I want to think this, anyway, because even Kaitlen Miller shouldn't be dead because I was too selfish to take this pill yesterday.

Casey's quiet. I look at him and try to feel what he's thinking. I feel my sternum, instead, rub the mummified pill nestled between my breasts. Maybe this will be a different kind of starting over than the bullet would have been. But I know now that was the only other way tonight could have ended.

Even if they've caught Dave by now, it doesn't change things. Dave's just one person; there are others, or there will be. Maybe Rick. Maybe Ellen, too. Maybe people I don't know yet. But I'm a target. Casey's a target, too, with me. And probably so many other people I don't care about right now who I should care about, who I *would* care about,

I hope, if I could think of anyone but myself and what I'm losing.

But for a little while here in the dark, feeling my hand in Casey's, I think I'd take this, hiding, forever.

I should let go of his hand, should say something. I *should* tell him everything. *Midnight,* I remind myself. By midnight, I will. Like I'll turn into a pumpkin or whatever then, and end this sick fairy tale. There always has to be a deadline, you know.

He pulls me back when some headlights swing around in our direction.

"Nate's car," he says then.

I follow his eyes to the overflow lot up the hill that's not lit up. When I squint, I can see Nate's black Focus where the pavement meets the treeline. I exhale. I didn't know I was holding my breath. "Thank goodness for parking," I say, and try to laugh, try to make something—anything—about this funny.

Casey looks at me. I guess this isn't the time for humor. But then he smiles.

So we hurry to the next tree, and then to the one after that. I think I should be tired, but I can feel my blood shimmying along my limbs, willing me to go faster.

"You're okay?" Casey asks, looking down at my feet. He's wanted to carry me since we got to the woods, but it's just mud, nothing sharp. It's like the ground here knew we were coming and was just waiting for us to run. Like everything else has fallen into place, all my good luck and this power I didn't ask for. And this will last, I know, until midnight. Because we have whatever is happening to me behind *us* now, wanting to save me right up until I won't let it anymore.

I haven't even broken a sweat by the time we get to the asphalt, and my breathing's even as we creep up to the driver's side of Nate's car. Casey fishes out a spare key from under the bumper and helps me inside. I crawl over the console, and then we're off without any headlights lighting our way to the road.

I'm finally out of breath when we're flying through the green light on Main. That's when I shift to get my seatbelt and find the umbrella in the way.

"You're okay?" Casey asks as he takes the bypass towards the highway. We're almost to the highway. The highway that will take us away. *Us*, still.

I hold up the umbrella. A chocolate smudge runs down one white triangle. There's a crack in the wood handle. I would have known it even if I hadn't had the dream so many times these last weeks.

"Yours?" I manage, finally, when we get off the ramp.

He nods.

I take his hand then and let the tears come as he keeps driving.

49

Casey

Mischa's quiet now. Maybe she's run out of tears. She doesn't say anything as we hand over our ID's to the man at the bus depot or as we pocket the tickets and I follow her out to the car rental down the street. We're leaving Nate's car here. It should make everyone think we left on a bus. To Denver, Mischa said, because she's always wanted to go. So her parents should buy this story, at least for a while.

It was my plan—the bus station, the tickets with Rick's credit card on the joint account Ellen has access to, and then using cash for a short-term car rental. More plan than I knew I had when we drove away from the school. More plan than I *should* have had, I think now, but I don't bother to ask where it came from. What matters is that we've disappeared, that Mischa's safe.

But she's still quiet. Too quiet for me to say I'll go get the rental car while she waits here, because I'm not sure that she won't disappear as soon as I'm not looking. There's some makeup smudged under her eyes, but she hasn't been crying for a while now.

She doesn't look at me anymore when I ask her if she's okay, when we—when *I*—talk through these plans. She just agrees. Which isn't Mischa. There's something wrong, something even bigger than having a crazed man trying to shoot her. Something bigger than running out of her junior prom, than running away.

We walk around the side of the car rental building to the restrooms, and I think through everything she's leaving behind, all the things that must add up. But none of these things are enough. Not for Mischa.

When she comes out a minute later, she's wiped off the makeup that was running under her eyes and redone her ponytail. I tell her how beautiful she looks, because I didn't say it enough before, and this woman in the dim glow of a security light is a Mischa I'll always remember, floating over the cracked asphalt in yellow satin with her eyes locked straight ahead of her like she's always known where she was going.

I follow her inside the rental office and up to a guy at the counter who's frowning at his phone. So he won't remember us. He doesn't even look at our ID's and takes the pile of cash without saying anything. They need a card to run in case there's damage, but it won't show up as a charge yet. I give him the company card for that, the one Rick uses for the dealership that Ellen doesn't have access to. Because he wants us to get away, I told Mischa. For tonight, at least. She nodded then like she believed me.

She's looking ahead when we go back outside, at the little blue sedan in lane four. For a second, I think she might grab the keys from me and take off with it on her own, but she gets in the passenger seat and lets me drive us back out into the darkness. She doesn't ask where we're going.

"There's a campground," I tell her when it's been quiet for too long. "An old one out past Kingston, by the river." It's a place I went in my life before, in what feels now like a different lifetime than the one with the Everfelds. "There's showers, and..." The road's quiet. I turn to look at Mischa. Her eyes are closed.

"They'll think we're on the bus," I tell her. "They'll go to Denver first."

She doesn't open her eyes.

The place is just fifteen minutes off the next exit, but it feels so much longer. When we pull in, I touch her hand.

She doesn't move away, at least.

There aren't any other cars, and I park all the way at the back of the camp behind some trees so nobody will be able to see us from the road.

Mischa's still quiet when we get out and walk to the concrete building they leave open all the time.

There's a bin of clothes from the lost and found like back when I needed them and showers and the sofa in the office where the manager let me sleep for a couple weeks when I was here the last time. The campground's closed until Memorial Day, but everything looks the same as when it was open.

I'm about to promise Mischa we'll get somewhere better soon, that our next place will have a bed and better food than we can get out of the vending machine with the dollars from Rick's wallet. But it's her sniffle that stops me.

When I turn back to her, she's standing in the doorway of the office. I move closer, hoping she'll fall into me instead of away, that at least she'll stay.

It takes her a while to say anything, but finally, there are words. Just not the ones I want to hear.

50

Mischa

I can't see well enough through my tears to really look at this place, to process this piece of Casey's past I want to know like I want to know all the pieces of Casey, all the time before and all the years after when I won't know him anymore.

Now, I just know enough to know that this isn't where he should be, that he deserves more than this place. He deserves more than to have gone through what he has already, too, more than to be running, but telling him this is a harder pill to swallow, as Mrs. Stevens would say, than the capsule nestled between my breasts. I tell myself I'd laugh at this irony another time and try to smile, but my face and my body are frozen in some state of grief for what hasn't even happened yet. Loss, I guess it is. Even if Casey is all I think about now when I think about what I'm losing.

I want to not face this, to just keep crying and let the clock run out and take the pill. But I owe him more than this. He has to go. Or one of us should, and I don't think I can make myself walk away from him.

Once I have my breath, I say this.

He doesn't move.

"You should go," I repeat, stronger this time as I look at my feet, at a pair of Nate's running shoes from his back seat, the laces pulled tight around my ankles.

"No," Casey says.

I look up. And then I'm sobbing again.

"Tell me you *want* me to go," he says when these sobs get stuck in my throat and I finally swallow them down like I will the pill. But the tears just keep coming, racing down my face and dripping into the neckline of my dress, being soaked up by the yellow satin like Kaitlen's blood was by hers. This will be like bleeding out, I think, in the end; the tears will soak through my dress and run down to the hem.

"Tell me that's what you want," Casey says again. "Tell me you want to do whatever it is you're going to do next without me, and I'll let you."

I can't do that, so I just say it again, that he *should* go, because I at least *want* to want him to be anywhere but here. I want to be a better person than I am right now. And when he reaches for my hand, I know I would take this pill a thousand times, that I would give up everything else with no regrets if I could just keep his hand through whatever comes next.

"Give me a reason," he says.

"That isn't..." I almost say 'fair,' but that's not right. What's happening to me isn't fair, either; I didn't ask for this, and it's not fair that I want what it's given me so much. Because I'm certain, whatever's brought us together, whatever's affecting me and whatever the pill that's digging into my heart does to stop it, this has changed me forever. Even if I don't take the pill, the *me* I was a month ago isn't the same me that's here now. This short time Casey's been in my life has changed me as much as a pill or a bullet ever could.

So I take the easy route, instead. I tell him why he couldn't come with me if I were going somewhere. Because of his scholarship—he'll get a full ride pretty much wherever he wants for baseball. Because of his team. Because of the Everfelds and all the other people in Centerville who care about him.

Casey reaches for my face. He keeps his hand there, my tears running over his fingers as he tries to get me to laugh by saying something about Rick trying to kill me—these are people he can leave behind, he tells me, the kind who would kill me, or at least who lend out their cars to someone who would.

I try to make myself laugh, but nothing gets past the ball in my throat, this bit of truth that's still stuck inside me.

"School," I manage after a second.

"We'll find a school," he says. "We can do that, can register on our own. Live on our own. We're seventeen."

He'd know, of course, at what age you don't need a guardian anymore. This is a history of Casey's I want to know, one I won't get a chance to even if I don't take this pill and run away, instead, like I'm letting him think I will.

"A good school," he says, "for you. And I'll work. We can do this."

We again. A *we* that can't be. A *we* that was all a trick, an illusion for him.

"We can do this," he repeats, closing the space between our bodies and wrapping me up in his arms like we're something real, like we could stay this way.

"No." I shake my head and tell myself that *I* can do this. I'll have to keep telling myself. "Dave meant to hit me, and now Kaitlen…"

"Kaitlen could be fine. You can't know she's…"

"It could have been you," I say. Because this was just a beginning. I wish I didn't know it, that I could argue myself out of it, rationalize some other reason for both cars and Sam Rodriguez turning blue at Mrs. Hoffman's feet and

Kaitlen lying in a puddle of her own blood in the middle of the gym floor. But I can't. Casey has to walk away now, and I have to take this pill. This is the only way out, the only way this will be over. For him, if for no one else, I have to take this pill.

His arms are squeezing me tight now, and I let myself breathe him in, my face smushed into the buttons on his shirt, my makeup smudging the crisp white cotton.

"I have to start over," I tell him—Dave's words, because I don't have any of my own left.

"*We* can start over," Casey whispers. "Rick, he's...he's going to let us go."

Us. "For now."

I feel his breath hitch, a shiver run through him that goes straight through me, too.

"Let me be with you," he says, his breath hot on my ear, his face wet against my forehead.

I swallow a sob as I try to memorize how this feels. His breath. The way his buttons are pressed into my cheek. This warmth, this *rightness* when I'm with him.

It takes me a while to force myself to step back. I can't look at him then, and my eyes land on the clock over the sofa. It's one of those big, cream-colored ones with a plastic bubble over it like Mr. Clark's history classroom had above the doorway in seventh grade, when I used to watch it at 11:36 every fourth period for Casey to pass by on his way to eat with the rest of the baseball team. They ate just before our lunch period to get to their workouts on time. That was his first year here. I remember how I always looked away, back at my notes or at Mr. Clark as soon as I saw Casey so he wouldn't know I was staring. Because this is one of those secrets you keep at thirteen, when you think you have so much time for secrets.

I wish now that I'd met his eyes, that I'd walked right up to him in the cafeteria when his lunch was ending and mine was beginning and told him then that we should be together for as long as we could.

But it's 11:47, so fast, and I owe him this. So I reach down my dress and fish out the tissue, damp with sweat and tears now, and I tell him everything.

51

Casey

I want to stop her, to tell her I don't need to hear this. I reach out and take the tissue from her, the one with the pill wrapped up inside. The pill she was going to take. *Is* going to take, if I can't stop her.

She lets it go. For now. She says midnight again, that this is when she's going to do it. I look at the clock. It's almost 11:58.

I can't get her to look at me, and probably she can't see, anyway, with the way she's crying, so I have to say it into her hair, have to squeeze my arms around her and hope she can feel somehow that I'm telling her the truth, that she should trust me.

I tell her I have dreams, too, and immediately wish I'd started with something else, since I'm trying to get her to believe I'm okay. But mine aren't really dreams; mine are awake, and chosen. Like I've chosen her, like I want so badly for her to choose me. It's probably too late now if she hasn't already.

Her hands fist on my shirt.

"I mean that I've felt it—what you're talking about," I tell her, "and I don't think it's bad."

She steps back this time. I want to stop her, to hold onto her.

But I let my arms fall. All I can do is keep talking, keep trying. "Did you ever do anything you didn't want to?" I ask before she can tell me she's already made up her mind. Before I really have to let her take this pill, if she thinks there's no other way out, because this is her choice, and what it does to me doesn't factor in.

But I'm selfish. Not like her. So I hurry the hell up. "You think *you* affected *me* with what's happening to you," I say, "but that couldn't have happened." Because Mischa Kenning-Elliott has been affecting me from the first moment I saw her. And I've known from that moment that this was my choice. So that's what I tell her.

I wish I'd found a way to know her a long time ago and convinced her years back that we could do this together, when it happened, that we would be in this together, whatever was going on around us. That we would *choose* each other, because this is our world, hers and mine, and nothing outside of it, outside of us, means anything.

She's looking at my hand with the tissue now. I want to squeeze it hard enough to burst the pill inside. I even want to take it myself. But this isn't what you do when you love someone, not for real. This isn't when you tell someone you love them, either. That's all I would say, over and over, until midnight or forever, if I thought it would make her stay.

Now, I don't say it even though I want to, even though I think it's the only thing that really matters. I tell her instead that I'm here, that this is where I want to be, where I *choose* to be, with her—wherever that ends up being. That I know it's up to her where she'll go next, and that if she goes somewhere without me, I'll follow her, stay away and do whatever I can to make sure she's safe without getting in her way. Whatever way that is. Whatever she finds out about what's affecting her. Whatever Ellen and Rick and Dave and god knows who else are trying to stop. None of them matter. Because this is something *right*, I tell her. And I'm sure, because it's Mischa. And the Mischa I know is right. The Mischa I love isn't controlled by anything.

She calls it a pull, like I've been pulled to her for forever. I tell her this again, that I've always known what she was, have always known somehow that this was what *we* were meant to be. But 'meant to be' isn't right; what I know now is that whatever's pulling either of us anywhere, I would choose this life with her without it, too.

She's quiet at 11:59. So here we are, waiting on the fat lady to sing. Waiting on Mischa, the way I think my whole life has been waiting on Mischa.

"Give me the pill," she says. Her voice is barely a whisper in my ear, and I hate myself for everything I think then. For how close I come to keeping it. For how close I come to throwing it out the window. For how close I come to taking it.

But I make my fist let go, make myself drop the wad of tissues into her palm and hope with everything I am that this isn't where we end.

52

Mischa

A shimmer on the wall catches my eye when I pull away from Casey. Moonlight. It takes a second for the plaque that caught it to come into focus.

Elkins Campground, 7205 North Culver Street.

I see the number clearly on the price tag on this dress, on my dashboard clock, and on my Thesis search as I walk to the bathroom, the wad of tissues clenched in my fist.

I'm seeing the pill clearly, too, when it's fizzling in the water of the toilet bowl. I press the lever to flush and watch it disappear.

Casey's standing behind me when I turn around, and I run into him then like he's what I've been running towards all this time, like I really can leave everything else behind me and keep this, keep who I am with him.

We don't talk about the thing anymore, about pull or

sway or influence or whatever it is that brought us here, to these numbers and these visions and each other. We don't talk about *meant to be*'s or my parents or Ellen or Rick or Dave. As we walk out to the pond where Casey used to watch minnows dart around the shallows, we talk instead about what we're choosing, about this life we're stepping into consciously, of our own free will. Wherever these next steps take us.

Casey wraps his arms around me as we lie back in the grass. I don't think about the mud on the yellow satin tangling in my legs then or about anything but how right this feels as I rest my head against his chest and dream of the Earth through a window, of how small we must look on that blue and green marble lost under the clouds.

Pull is the first novel in a series whose universe is shared with A.C. Rob's forthcoming *Rock* series. To subscribe for updates on the next installment or to contact Jaime, please visit jaimewinn.com.